D0775512

Sign up for book announcements and special deals at:

AWBALDWIN.COM

G. W. Baldwin

ACCLAIM FOR THE

RELIC SERIES NOVELS

BY AWARD WINNING AUTHOR
A.W. BALDWIN

DESERT GUARDIAN

A moonshining hermit.
A campus bookworm.
A midnight murder.

Ethan's world turns upside-down when he slips off the edge of red-rock cliffs into a world of twisting ravines and coveted artifacts. Saved by a mysterious desert recluse named Relic, Ethan must join a whitewater rafting group and make his way back to civilization. But someone in the gorge is killing to protect their illegal dig for ancient treasures... When Anya, the lead whitewater guide, is attacked, he must divert the killer into the dark canyon night, but his most deadly pursuer is not who he thinks... Ethan struggles to save his new friends, face his own mortality, and unravel the chilling murders. But when they flee the secluded canyon, a lethal hunter is hot on their trail...

Can an unlikely duo and a whitewater crew save themselves and an ancient Aztec battlefield from deadly looters?

RAPTOR CANYON

A moonshining hermit.
A big city lawyer.
A $35 million con job.

An impromptu murder leads a hermit named Relic to an unlikely set of dinosaur petroglyphs and to swindlers using the unique rock art to turn the canyon into a high-end tourist trap. Attorney Wyatt and his boss travel to the site to approve the next phase of financing, but his boss is not what he seems... When a treacherous security chief tries to kill Relic, Wyatt is caught in the deadly chase. The mismatched pair must tolerate each other while fleeing through white-water rapids, remote gorges, and hidden caverns. Relic devises a plan to save the treasured canyon, but Wyatt must come to terms with the cost to his career if he fights his powerful boss... A college student with secret ties to the site, Faye joins the kitchen crew so she can spy on the enigmatic project. When she hears Relic's desperate plan, she has a decision to make...

Armed with a full box of toothpicks (and a little dynamite), can the unlikely trio monkey-wrench the corrupt land deal and recast the fate of Raptor Canyon?

"A gem of a read…"
> – **_Dirk Cussler_**, #1 New York Times
> best-selling Author

"[You'll be] holding your heart and your breath at the same time…"
> – **_Peter Greene_**, award winning author of the
> _Adventures of Jonathan Moore_ series

"A hoot of an adventure novel…"
> – **_Reader's Favorite, Five Star Review._**

Grand Master Adventure Writers' Finalist Award 2019

ScreenCraft Cinematic Book Contest Finalist 2019-2020

BUY NOW
FROM A BOOKSTORE NEAR YOU OR
AMAZON.COM

WINGS OVER GHOST CREEK

A moonshining hermit.
A reluctant pilot.
A $5 million plunder.

Owen discovers a murdered corpse at a college-run archeological dig in the Utah outback but when he and a park service pilot try to reach the sheriff for help, their plane is shot from the sky. Owen must ditch the aircraft in the Colorado River, where he is saved by a gin-brewing recluse named Relic. The offbeat pair flee from the sniper and circle back to warn the students but not everyone there is who they seem... The two must trek through rugged canyon country, unravel a baffling mystery, and foil a remarkable form of thievery. Suzy, a student at the dig, helps spearhead their escape but the unique team of crooks has a surprise for them...

Can they uncover the truth and escape an archeology field class that hides assassins and dealers in black-market treasure?

"A beautifully written thriller."
    – *Readers' Favorite Five Star Review*

"[A] humorous, fun, and well-plotted adventure. Baldwin is a master storyteller…"
    – *Landon Beach*, Bestselling Author of *The Sail*

"Baldwin delivers another gripping Relic tale with trademark wit and deft expression. This is adventure with philosophy that keeps you nodding your head long after you've put the book down."
    – *Jacob P. Avila*, *Cave Diver*, Grand Master Adventure Writers Award Winner

Wings offers "…action-packed adventure and nerve-racking suspense, with a touch of romance and humor mixed in." Baldwin has a "gift for capturing the reader's attention at the beginning and keeping them spellbound"
    – *Onlinebookclub.org review*

Grand Master Adventure Writers' Finalist Award

BUY NOW
FROM A BOOKSTORE NEAR YOU OR AMAZON.COM

DIAMONDS OF DEVIL'S TAIL

A moonshining hermit.
An English major.
A $4 million jewel heist.

When diamonds appear in a remote canyon stream, whitewater rafters and artifact thieves set off in a deadly race to the source.

Brayden, an aspiring writer, works in a Chicago insurance firm with his ambitious uncle when they embark on a wilderness whitewater adventure. On a remote hike, they find their colleague, Dylan, dead in the sand, a handful of gems in his fist. When thieves charge in, Brayden flees deeper into the canyon, where he encounters a gin-brewing recluse named Relic. Brayden's uncle is cornered and cuts a deal with the thieves, but they each have a surprise for the other... and the rafters have ideas of their own about getting rich quick... Brayden and Relic must become allies, traverse the harsh desert, and beat the thieves to the hidden gems. Brayden must confront his uncle about suspicious payments at their insurance firm and what he was really doing at the stream where Dylan was killed…

Can they discover the truth, find the lost jewels, and protect the rafters from grenade-tossing thieves?

"…an adeptly written thriller…the excitement and tension are superb…the entire plot [is] compelling"
    – Readers' Favorite Five Star Review

"straightforward and thrilling, with humor intermixed… Relic is a unique and intriguing character…passionately interested in preserving the ancient archeological sites and conserving the land and water…[We] enthusiastically recommend it to readers who enjoy thrillers, action-packed adventure, and crime novels."
    – Onlinebookclub.org four out of four Star Review

"Another rollicking Relic ride from A.W. Baldwin…a bunch of double-crossing, dirt dealing, diamond thieves run into Relic's trademark wit and ingenuity. Enjoy!"
    – Jacob P. Avila, *Cave Diver*, Grand Master Adventure Writers Award Winner

BUY NOW

FROM A BOOKSTORE NEAR YOU OR

AMAZON.COM

A.W. BALDWIN
BROKEN INN

ISBN   978-1-7353626-4-9 Hardbound
ISBN   978-1-7353626-5-6 Paperback
ISBN   978-1-7353626-6-3 ebook

Cover art by Daniel Thiede.
Map art by Nathan Baldwin.

For Julie, Gregg, Debbie, Mike, Gail, Mark, and Craig

Gravel road

Demon's Roost canyon

Trail

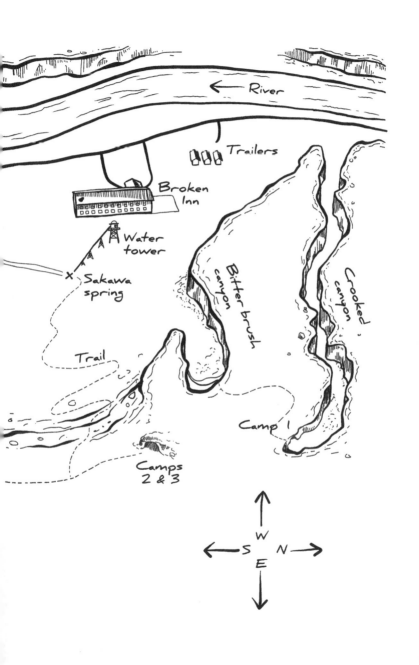

CHAPTER 1

"Well, butter my buns…"

He shaded his eyes with the palm of his hand.

There were two pickup trucks in Demon's Roost canyon – one in the deep arroyo at the base of sheer cliffs to the south, one on the upper flats that made up most of the corkscrew canyon. There'd been uranium mining here in the 1950s, but what these yahoos were doing now was a mystery.

Relic tightened his ponytail and stared into the twisting gorge.

Yesterday morning, snow capped the hoodoos – white icing on scarlet cupcakes. By this afternoon, the sun-fired rocks had begun radiating heat near 100 degrees, wringing moisture from the human body like a twisted sponge. The cliffs above him seemed to glow, slivers of clay injected into the blood-red sandstone like fat marbled into raw steak. A pair of crows squawked overhead.

An unlikely descendent of disparate clansmen —
one Scottish, one Hopi — Relic wandered these plateaus
and chasms, a sometimes-trespasser, recluse, and moonshiner. He'd been called a vagabond, a sasquatch of the
desert, but these remote places were home.

He left his pack by a rock and trotted down the trail
to the bottom of the canyon. He moved quickly around
the first bend to a spot close to the truck on the flats. No
one seemed to be around. He walked to the pickup, a
silver double-cab, its tailgate down. Topographic maps
lay flattened across the truck bed, rocks on the corners to
hold them in place. An empty five-gallon container for
water sat on the end of the tailgate, neon-orange stripes
across its side. A gust of wind slid the plastic canister off
the edge and Relic picked it up.

The maps were of Demon's Roost and places to
the north. Scribbles and circles were penciled over the
contour lines, but he couldn't tell what they meant. The
second truck, the one in the dry creek bed, sat around a
bend in the canyon, out of sight from this position.

Something made him uneasy. Some distant vibration, maybe. The crows had gone silent. Charcoal clouds
hung in the east.

Two men rounded the corner, boots rasping over
the sand, heads down, mumbling to each other. He

watched from behind the silver truck, some fifteen feet above them and thirty yards away. One wore jeans and a white dress shirt, out of place in this remote canyon. The other wore a red shirt with a leather strap across his shoulder.

Relic took a step back and felt it again – this time a deep rumble under his boots – and suddenly he knew what was coming. Though desperately dry, it was water that had shaped these desert lands, sheer bluffs and jagged drainages wrought by the power of rain. A cloudburst 50 miles away could become a flash flood in these narrow canyons, a deadly blast of water exploding with little warning. The men in the arroyo stood directly in its path.

"Hey, hey!" Relic raised the empty water container above his head, waving it in the air, sprinting past the pickup truck and toward the edge of the ravine.

One of the men looked up.

"Get out of there! Out of there!" Relic shouted, pointing up the embankment, urging them to run from the dry creek bed before it was too late.

The other man straightened, suddenly startled, and reached for his side.

"Flash flood! Flash flood!" Relic waved the plastic canister again and stepped to the edge of the ravine.

The dissonance in his toes became a bellow in his

head, an angry groan.

One man began to climb from the bottom of the arroyo, boots slipping up the sandy rise. The other lifted his hand from his side, a pistol in his fingers, aiming it toward Relic.

Relic spiraled backward reflexively, stepping suddenly into thin air, dropping down the slope, skidding feet-first through loose sand all the way to the bottom. He stood and looked at the gunman, who'd holstered his pistol and begun climbing the side of the arroyo behind his companion. In a moment, they both stood above the empty drainage, out of danger.

Now the sound of thunder rolled through the canyon, echoes doubling the alarm. Relic ran down the dry bed, frantically searching its steep walls for a place he could ascend. The rumble became the roar of whitewater, ramjet engines at full throttle, all other sound blasted aside by the urgency and enormity of the coming flood.

Relic turned in time to see a two-foot bank of water rise behind him, precursor to the deluge to come.

He held tight to the empty container and ran toward the spot the two men had used to climb from the dry bed, but as he began to scramble up the slope, the coffee-colored water, heavy with silt, reached his feet, sweeping them forward, twisting him down into the roiling river.

He wrapped his arms around the canister, his make-shift life vest, and lifted his feet in front of him. A surge forced him underwater – his eyes closed, mouth shut – then lifted him rapidly toward the top of the arroyo, shoving him forward faster than a man could run. He kicked to keep his feet downstream, buffers against rocks, trees, or cliffs. The newborn river hurtled him around the bend, a choleric infant wailing at the world.

The second pickup truck lay directly in his path.

He wiggled and twisted, paddling his boots as fast as he could, but the truck came swiftly closer, closer, his feet about to smash into the rear window. If he were forced through the glass and into the cab of the truck, the river would pin him there and drown him. But as he approached, he seemed to slow, then slow some more. His boots touched the window. He bent his knees and pushed away, then he realized he hadn't slowed at all. The truck had been lifted from the ground and shoved forward with him. The water carried them both through the flood together.

The deluge raged around another bend in the canyon, rocks clacking violently against each other along the bottom, tumbling into the flow from the sides, debris that could crush him in a second if he got caught between them. The truck separated from him, rolling to its side. A wave suddenly tossed his head and chest above the flow, his feet pulled downward. He flipped forward and under the rapids, no time to take a breath. Despite the buoyancy of the canister, the swirling river forced him downward, somersaulting into the dark. He lost all sense of direction, what was up or down, dizzy in the swirling storm, helpless under the unyielding, raging current. Pressure rose in his lungs to near explosion, his diaphragm tensing, preparing to blow his final breath from his chest, when finally he spun upward, his head breaking through, and he gasped.

He pushed on the container, lifting his head as high as he could, hungrily sucking in air. The sides of the arroyo sped by, bending left, then right, disorienting him. His boots struck something hard, and he realized his legs were dangling below him again – a dangerous position. He pulled himself into a back float, feet downstream, arms clutching the canister. Waves splashed into his eyes and mouth, blinding him for seconds at a time, forcing him to take quick, shallow breaths. The current threatened to spin him again, so he paddled his feet, twisting to keep his face above water.

The waves began to spread farther apart and his sight improved when he squinted. The truck was behind him now, spinning slowly in the current as he passed another bend in the gorge.

The sky seemed to lighten as the canyon walls receded. He felt his elevation lower as the flood spread across more open ground, closer to its destination in the Colorado River.

He spun to his left and kicked as hard as he could, moving out of the current. In moments, his bottom touched hard ground. He pushed farther away from the receding water until he could sit up. A three-inch flow continued to swirl around him, but he knew he was safe.

He took full, deep breaths, clearing the adrenaline from his system, regaining a sense of balance.

The flow of water slowly turned to mud. The truck had rounded the last corner, then gotten stuck behind a rock and buried nearly a foot deep in the sandy bottom. He dropped the empty container and wiped the water and hair from his eyes.

"This is the worst thing that's happened since the last thing," he told himself with a grin. It was the second time he'd been caught in a flash flood and nearly drowned. The first time, it'd been his own damn fault. Well, hell, he thought, maybe it was his own fault this time, too.

If the swim hadn't been so deadly, part of him, at

least, could have admitted to the thrill.

He sat for a moment, staring into the clear sky. Who were those guys and what the hell were they doing in this canyon? And why did one of them draw his pistol when he'd warned them about the flood?

"I guess no good deed goes unpunished," he scolded himself. He stood slowly, shaking out his arms and legs. He removed his shirt, wrung it out, and put it back on. "I'll dry you out later," he spoke to his pants and boots.

It was time to get the hell out of there.

CHAPTER 2

After 41 years, Edward was finally going to dump this baggage on someone else, some other schmuck who would not realize the hopelessness of the investment. Three friends had tried to make a go of the hotel. He'd invested, too. But in the end, after a contentious bankruptcy, he was the major creditor and the one who'd ended up with the title to the property. Well, they were no longer friends, and he'd become the schmuck-in-chief, the partner with the weight around his neck.

He glanced in the mirror behind the bar. His belly seemed larger than it last did, maybe distorted in the cheap reflection, his hair a dirty shade of snow. He'd stopped shaving, allowing the stubble to lengthen, hiding the folds of age on his neck. He straightened his tie and moved to the booth in the back, the place Mr. Smith had said they should meet at five o'clock.

He slid his briefcase onto the seat next to him

and waited.

A short, buxom waitress moved listlessly from table to table, wiping the stains with a fatal boredom, unthinking and perfunctory. He waved two fingers to get her attention, but she ignored him entirely.

Someone entered the bar, just then, out of his line of sight. The waitress stood suddenly alert, the rag now held behind her back, and she smiled and nodded a greeting as a man in a dark jacket and brimmed hat walked inside. Without breaking stride, he turned and headed toward the booth, a man who knew exactly where he was going.

"Mr. Smith?" Edward rose and offered his hand.

Smith shook it quickly, a tight, hard grip, and turned to the waitress, who'd followed him. "My usual," he said.

She waited a beat.

"Bourbon and water," Edward said. "No ice."

Smith removed his hat and slid into the seat, nut-brown eyes lackluster and barren. His hair was graying at the temples, worry lines etched in his face, but he moved like a man who worked out at the gym – sturdy and confident.

The waitress set their drinks on the table and walked away.

"Nice little bar."

"It belongs to a friend." Smith folded his hands in front of his drink. "Good place for some business."

Edward nodded, a drop of sweat rolling from the pit of his arm. Two men wandered to the bar and leaned on stools, watching the place. One of them was huge. A young couple sat at a table across the room, but otherwise the pub was empty.

"Got the lease?"

He pulled the papers from his briefcase – a lease with an option to purchase, an option he fervently hoped they would exercise. "Just as you said, made out to J and J Investments." He handed it across the table.

Smith examined the document.

"All you have to do is record it – file it – with the county records."

"Right," Smith said absentmindedly.

The two men at the bar watched them.

"Hey, uh…." He pointed toward the men.

Without looking up, Smith nodded. "They're with me. This is in good order, I see." He pushed the lease to the side, reached into his jacket pocket, and pulled out an envelope. He handed it to Edward, his eyes dark and implacable, an empty chalkboard.

Inside was a wad of cash. He flipped through the

bills, counting them in his head. Ten thousand dollars. Only a quarter of what it should be.

"Hey...." Edward looked up at Smith, who waved a finger at the men at the bar. They moved quickly to the table. The giant of a man had a large, misshapen nose and his suit pulled tight when he flexed his shoulders. He made the other guy look like a skinny teenager.

Smith tilted his head and clasped his hands together.

"This is not what we agreed to." Edward swallowed hard, glancing from Smith to the hulk and back to Smith. Another drop of sweat rolled down his side.

Smith spread his hands. "After a thorough review of the situation, we have determined that the amount in that envelope is exactly what the signing bonus should be. As agreed, you will earn one percent of our gross profits per year, if there are any, up to 3,000 dollars a month in rental payments. Like we discussed on the phone, the signing bonus is not part of the written lease. Think of it as a token of our generosity."

"But—"

"We had our appraisers out there two weeks ago. Flash flood nearly took them out. There's nothing there but a dilapidated old inn and a few miles of dirt road. And a bunch of rocks."

"There's a nice little spring...."

"Are you challenging the determination of the value of this deal by my colleagues?" Smith wrapped one hand around a fist and stared into Edward's eyes. "They are highly skilled and experienced."

"No doubt, but, well, I was just surprised by this."

"I understand. Take a drink and consider the situation for a moment."

He could use a drink right now, and more than one, but not with these men hovering over him.

Damn it. He should have known better. He did know better, in fact. He'd wanted so badly to believe the deal was on the up-and-up that he'd moved forward despite his doubts. But there was nothing in writing about the signing bonus. No appraisal, no bankers, no escrow, no lawyers, just an agreement to deliver a signed lease at five o'clock in this lonely little bar in the industrial district. Of course there was going to be a catch.

The man standing across from Edward blocked his view of the rest of the bar. He could break any bone he chose in Edward's body, one by one. That guy knew it. Edward knew it. Smith knew it.

These guys were organized crime, he realized, here and now, in the modern era. Commercial leases. Property acquisitions. Dummy corporations. Some legitimate rent would be paid to Edward, an amount that lawyers could argue about for years, an amount a court might well decide was reasonable in today's real estate market.

What did these guys want with the old Broken Inn, anyway? It bordered a short stretch of the Colorado River, but its water rights had been abandoned even before the bankruptcy. Like Smith had said, it was basically a pile of rocks.

Damn it. He could really use the whole amount, the $40,000 as agreed on the phone. He had other business concerns that would benefit from an infusion of cash. But there was the potential for a sale and regular monthly rental income from the lease. At least that much was in writing. And maybe he was getting greedy. The property was a drag on his personal economy and in his heart, he knew he'd take even less than Smith's cash, if necessary. Especially if the deal ensured he'd walk out of the room on his own two feet, no broken hands or ribs – or worse.

He stared into the honey-colored bourbon and finally nodded.

Smith slid the lease into his coat pocket, twisting his lips in what would not quite pass for a smile, even for him. Smith tossed the drink down his throat. The two men stepped away, making room for him to stand.

"And you are satisfied that we have been fair and

just with you?" Smith slid his hat onto his head.

"Yes."

"Our business is done here, right?" Smith straightened his jacket.

"Yes, of course," Edward's voice creaked. "All done."

CHAPTER 3

SIX WEEKS LATER

Hailey hurriedly checked herself in the mirror, her hair a cinnamon brunette, her eyes like her mother's — earthen brown and blessed with naturally long lashes. She smacked her lips together, testing the clear gloss, and smoothed a denim shirt over her slight frame. She saw her mother in her reflection again, and a wave of loneliness swept through her. She bit her lower lip until the pain distracted her.

She was due to meet with her college advisor, Carol, right after the "Careers in Writing" class that Carol taught. Hailey was running late. She grabbed a rain jacket and hurried from her small apartment.

A steady mist filled the air, soaking her coat with cold precipitation, Seattle's pre-spring melancholy stealing the sky from view.

Her mother had died four months before, nearly to the day. The sudden loss had put her in a spin, and though she felt like she'd recovered from the worst of it, a ragged sadness still stopped her cold and an unchecked anger still shot her forward, the oscillation between them exhausting. Journalism had been her major and her passion, but now, even with a simple progression of facts, she just did not know how to write the story.

She entered the main building and moved past the wandering students to the doorway for room 115. Inside, the lecture hall sat empty but for Carol, leaning on the lectern at the head of the class.

Hailey started down the steps. "Sorry I'm late."

"You look like you're still underwater."

"I know." She slipped out of her raincoat.

"Soaked in and weighed down."

"Yeah." Hailey shook the jacket, spreading raindrops over an empty chair.

"Maybe it's the weather that's gotten into you."

"Maybe."

"Weeks of dreariness slowing you down," Carol nodded.

"Hey…"

"It hits the best of us, sometimes."

"What?"

"I'm just saying…"

"Are we still talking about the weather?" Hailey asked.

"You're just not following through these days." Carol squinted at her, a gentle accusation. "You've worked so hard to get this far. Don't quit on yourself."

"I am not a quitter." Hailey forced the words through her teeth.

"You didn't used to be." Carol spoke through clamped lips.

"Now you're mocking me?" Hailey pulled her chin to her chest. "You're supposed to be my friend."

"I am your friend." Carol crossed her arms. "But I'm your faculty advisor, too, and I want to see you finish this – get your degree. With honors."

Hailey stared toward the cinderblock wall as if to see right through it.

"You're short the special project credits."

"I've got the grades."

"Your research on presidential press coverage is completely AWOL."

"To hell with it." Hailey swatted the air.

"Listen," Carol scooted closer to her, "you've had a terrible loss. I lost my mom five years ago—"

"Not to Covid."

"It's been months."

Hailey narrowed her eyes, anger surfacing.

"Listen, I just want to see you succeed. But right now, you're in some kind of morass. I've watched you try to decide whether to be on time for class." Carol shook her head. "Hell, you'd let indecision run your life, but you're not sure whether to let it." She smiled crookedly.

"I've tried." Hailey hung her head. "I don't know what to do next. And I'm out of money. My loans are used up. Rent is due in 10 days. I've got to get a paying job." The only thing she owned was her old Chevy Blazer and its transmission was starting to slip. Like her ability to move forward.

"Listen, I know all that, and I've had an idea. Drop the whole research project. I know you need work, a paying gig. There's a little-used externship program the university sponsors. The college subsidizes most of the salary. A small newspaper hires you and covers its own expenses. You write for them for a semester – two if you decide you like it. The project supports local papers and helps get students or new grads into the field."

Hailey stared at her shoes, flats she'd bought on her last shopping trip with her mother.

"It's good experience."

"Covering bake sales and dog catchers?"

"Seeing the business side of running a newspaper, learning how local boards work – or don't work – covering all the beats all the time instead of specializing."

"Sounds exciting." She heard the sarcasm leaking from her voice.

"You told your mom you'd graduate, and that you'd do it with honors."

"You're using that against me?" Hailey stiffened.

"I'm not using anything against you. You're my friend. With this project, you can graduate. It's enough for your final credits and will let me get you that special status. Plus, you'll have real experience on your resumé."

She stayed quiet for a moment.

Carol sat back. "Hailey, it's time to take it or leave it."

She rubbed her brow.

"And it's not much, but there is a paycheck."

"Where?"

"The job's in Utah."

"Jeez, Carol – could you find something farther from home?"

"The closer slots have already been taken. But this place is near national parks like Arches and Canyonlands."

"Oh, god. A journalist's dead end."

"Not at all. And it's beautiful country out there.

Frank and I went after his sister died. We'll do a short video interview with the editor, then he'll set you up with a payroll advance and a place to live."

Hailey patted her hands on her knees, a nervous habit.

"So, what's it gonna be?" Carol asked.

"Seems like the decision's already made."

"Atta girl."

CHAPTER 4

"Why can't stupidity be painful?"

This had to be connected with those two yahoos Relic had saved from the flash flood at Demon's Roost, the next canyon south.

He set his pack behind a rock and stared at the desert spring, its sweet water sucked nearly to the bottom of the muddy banks. A black hose choked the little water hole, oppressing it for the pump above, forcing it over a knoll and into a wider tube that stretched across the ground.

Lines were etched in a flat stone above: an upside-down loop, the bottom split and opened inward. The ancient petroglyph served as a symbol of the life provided by this little oasis.

"Snotheads." Relic trotted to the gasoline engine working the pump. He removed the air filter, set it aside, and scooped some dust into the palm of his hand. He stood over the open carburetor and poured the fine dirt into it until the engine sputtered, misfired, and shuddered to a stop. A breeze cleared the air of exhaust.

He wiped his hands on his pants and decided to put the air filter back onto the ruined engine, hiding the cause of its demise. He stretched his arms and looked back along a narrow game trail he'd used to climb from the plateau above to the natural shelf where Sakwa Spring rested. Someone had made a terrible mess of it.

He followed the pumping tube a few yards to the edge of a lip, where the flexible rubber joined a solid PVC pipe, one end anchored to the ground. Extending across a long dip in the terrain, the pipe was supported by fresh pine posts and one-by-six braces – giant popsicle sticks crisscrossed against each other, cradling the PVC until it reached an elevated metal water tower. The top of the tower was open, maybe 20 feet across, and a little above the spot where he stood. Beneath the cistern, another pipe reached down the metal supports and along the ground, leading toward the old, abandoned Broken Inn.

Not deserted anymore.

He moved down the slope and past the tower to a flat spot nearly three-quarters of a mile above the inn. He knelt in the dirt and pulled his ponytail to the side. He'd left his southern camp that morning, twelve hard miles from here.

And his water bottle was empty.

The old inn had seen better days, its siding dried to the color of bone by the harsh desert sun, the roof sagging along its ribs. A hole had poked through its shake shingles on the southern end. But farther down the building, new plywood covered the canopy, straight and steady, repaired and waiting for modern roofing. The structure was two stories high, ten boarded-up windows staring blindly at him along each floor. To the north, he could see temporary walls low to the ground that would shape an expanded concrete foundation.

The sound of boots on hardscrabble reached his ears, suddenly close and full of confidence. Someone must have been waiting around the bend, watching over the site. Someone heavy.

"Hey! What are you doing up here?"

CHAPTER 5

Her view vibrated with the bicycle tires like a rolling, split-screen movie: a sandstone trail to her right, close-up and clear, a rugged canyon to her left, distant and washed out of focus. She'd lost the main trail, following an ever-dimming path that took her along a bench of rock, closer and closer to the cliff's edge.

Hailey squeezed her brakes to a full stop.

The Colorado River wound its way from the north through a wide swath of canyon on either side. The rim ended three yards away from her, dropping hundreds of feet to a relatively flat basin the river had carved eons ago from solid rock.

The abrupt edge and soaring height made her a little dizzy.

She'd moved from Seattle two days ago and already yearned for the smell of saltwater and fish. She missed Pike Place Market, the busy streets, tall, glassy buildings, restaurants, nightclubs. The gossip among reporters, the chance to read and write stories that influenced the fate of policies and politicians, the chance to be at the center of it all.

This red rock country felt like the middle of nowhere. Downtown Mars, in fact. On someone's advice, she'd bought a guidebook to the area, but now she scoffed at the thought. Had she expected to find trolley routes, live theaters, or import shops in this dusty place?

She dismounted too quickly and fell awkwardly to the ground, scraping her leg against a stone as she went. Damn it. Her calf bled for a moment. She lifted and re-laid her rented bike on its side, nervous about moving any closer to the edge. She found a stool-sized rock and settled onto it, feeling solid ground beneath her, soothing her sense of vertigo.

She was done with this whole mountain bike experiment. She'd walk it back to her Blazer, toss it in the rear, and return to her small apartment in town. When she'd rented the place, the owner had said it was on Main Street, overlooking city hall and a public park. That had soothed her fears. But when she arrived, she saw that Main Street was only a half-mile long, the park a tiny fountain with no water in it, and the entire city government stuffed into a shallow row of stucco offices. It seemed like the whole town would fit inside Lander Hall, her first-year dormitory at the University of Washington.

She removed her small day pack and took a long drink of water.

She remembered her job interview with Mr. Martineau, the editor of the local paper. He'd said she would be covering community events, local business-es, and some of their honored citizens. She'd wanted to gag. Human-interest stories – pot roasts and bake sales. The place was a career killer, a no man's land. But there was little she could do about it now.

Tomorrow would be the first of the month and her first day on the new job. Martineau had urged her to rent a mountain bike and binoculars and start see-ing the canyon country she'd be writing about. Back home, she'd been on day hikes on Snow Lake and Nis-qually trails with an old boyfriend, but the paths were busy, heavily used by others. Today, she found herself all alone in the desert outback. When she'd accidental-ly taken the path less traveled, it had gotten downright spooky. She'd get back to the main trail soon, cut back up or backtrack if she had to.

She stared across the open expanse, past the Colorado River and into the dusty horizon. The rumble of diesel engines and the random clangs of construction drew her attention closer at hand, to an area just south of her perch along the canyon rim. An aging wooden building was the focus of human activity below. It sat some distance from the water, not far from where the canyon walls began to rise. She put the binoculars to her eyes.

Her guidebook said the building was called the Broken Inn, a 1950s-era retreat renovated in the1970s, then abandoned again to the sand and wind. The private land remained that way, grandfathered in when the canyons surrounding it were incorporated into the national park. The name had something to do with wild horses being saddle-broken there at one time. She noticed a gaping hole in the roof of the original section, on the southern end, the name of the place now fitting for other reasons.

But fresh walls ran along the side, part of some new renovation, she assumed. Short plywood braces enclosed an area along the northern end of the building. A grid of wire and rebar spread across the ground there, apparently to become the footing and floor for an expansion. A concrete mixer truck spun without urgency, waiting to slide its load into one corner of the new foundation.

A man in a white dress shirt, out of place among the workers, walked toward the truck, spinning his right hand in the air. Workers stopped what they were doing and hustled away from the site. The driver hopped out of the truck and joined the others as they went down a dirt road toward a row of three trailers positioned close to the river.

She rested her elbows on her knees and refocused the binoculars, taking in the show. There wasn't anything better to do.

Two men stayed behind with the man in the white shirt. One sat in the dirt amidst the grid of rebar, an odd place to be, gesturing something, shaking his head. One of the men, a taller guy, wandered about, watching the other workers stroll down a dip in the road, headed for the trailer houses. It was nearly noon; maybe they were on a lunch break.

The man in the white shirt rolled up his sleeves and motioned to the wandering man, who strode to the cement truck and climbed in.

She tried to focus on the face of the man who seemed to be in charge, but the image was blurry at this distance. The man in the dirt stood up, gesturing again, something urgent. The man in the white shirt pulled a pistol from behind his back and aimed it at the standing man, who suddenly stopped all movement.

Her breath stuck in her throat.

The man with the pistol moved close to the other and placed the gun against the side of his forehead. The man's head bounced unnaturally against his shoulder, his neck bones suddenly liquid, his joints gummy, and he collapsed back to the ground. The sound of a muffled pop reached her ears seconds later.

Holy shit.

She focused for a moment on the rumpled mass of humanity, clothed in a blue work shirt and jeans, absolutely immobile. She couldn't make out his face. She moved her view back to the man in the white dress shirt, who stepped even closer to the man he'd shot. He wiped the pistol with a rag, held it over the body, and let it drop. His foot pushed the man's shoulder, flattening him against the ground, then he stepped carefully out from the grid of rebar.

The man in the white shirt circled his arm in the air again and the sound of the concrete truck choked, clutch in, clutch out, changing the turn of the spiral blade so it pushed concrete out of the drum. She watched as the cement sloughed through the chute and spread across the corner foundation, swamping the body.

In moments, the scene was tranquil again, the man in the shirt unrolling his sleeves, walking away. The man in the truck came out and lifted a pole with a slat on the end. He began shifting and smoothing the concrete into a uniform mass, gray as the grave it had become.

CHAPTER 6

Relic turned to look.

"What are you doing here?"

The man stood over six foot five inches tall, his chest like a bulging suitcase, biceps meaty as pot roasts. A nightstick hung like a sword on one side of his belt; a walkie-talkie hung on the other. His nose was a bulbous marble, misshapen, out of place in the middle of an angular skull. An old wrestling injury, maybe. His pale eyes began to squint, suspicion tightening his face.

Relic rose slowly.

"Juan?" The voice came from below them.

Relic and the giant stared at each other.

"Juan, we need you down here!" A worker with short, dark hair waved at Relic. "¡Vena qui abajo!"

Relic saw the opportunity presented by the worker, and by his question. "¿Que?" he asked the giant.

"¡Andale!" shouted the worker from below.

Relic turned quickly and slid down the slope, away from the gringo who'd confronted him.

The worker cuffed Relic's head lightly and launched into a tirade of Spanish Relic could not translate. But the meaning was clear: this fellow had saved his skin, rebuking him for being away from the work site, leading him away from the round-nosed giant.

Relic played along, shuffling ahead until they were out of hearing range. They walked quietly a little farther, moving past the old part of the inn, toward the renovated section.

"English?" Relic asked.

"Sí." The man wore a deep tan, his face wide and friendly. Gray hair peppered his temples.

"Relic." He offered his hand. "Or maybe, Juan…"

"Manny." He shook Relic's hand and grinned. "You look like you could use a meal. And a shower."

Relic looked intently at Manny, his question implicit.

"That side of beef is dangerous, man. Loco. I did not want to clean up the mess after he beat the crap out of you."

"Gracias." Relic tucked his hands in his pockets. "I need water."

"Follow me. We will go to the kitchen, where the

crew is eating now."

"You can get me in there?"

"I will say you are my brother-in-law, Juan, here to help unload the cinder blocks."

"I owe you, my friend."

"Sí, and you will have to move some cinder blocks, too. We are short on help here."

"I expect to work for my supper – no handouts."

"No handouts."

"What do you do here?"

"I am a carpenter. I also oversee the new addition to the old inn, and I manage the other carpenters and the laborers. Like you." His lip rose in a quick grin.

Relic nodded.

"We work hard here, ten and twelve-hour days, then stay in rooms in these trailers." He pointed. "One trailer is a kitchen, two trailers have rooms for the men. The smaller one has showers in the back."

"How long have they been taking water out of the little spring up there?"

"A while now. They use it to mix with the concrete."

"Why not take water from the river?"

Manny shrugged. "I heard they need permission from the government. A permit. A bigger pump. Who knows? And, for now, they filter it for showers and the septic system for us. The drinking water, they haul that in."

The road to the trailers dipped steadily closer to the river. Relic glanced upward as they passed the work site. He could hear a cement truck gunning its engine, probably churning the stuff for the expanded foundation.

The smell of roasting beef reached his nose and his stomach grumbled.

For now, he was sticking with Manny.

CHAPTER 7

Hailey moved her binoculars from her eyes and stared at the distant construction site.

Damn.

She put the field glasses back into her pack and patted her knees with her hands.

"What do I do now?"

Take one step at a time, she told herself. Cell phone service is spotty out here, so just wait on that. Get back onto the main trail. Ride back to the Blazer, load up, and return the bike and binoculars to the rental shop. Go to the police. No. Go to her editor, Mr. Martineau. What if he didn't believe her? Some big-city girl with a bunch of crazy ideas, searching for a big story as soon as she got here? Making it all up to satisfy her ambition?

Crap.

He'd have to believe her, he'd just have to. At least he'd know what to do next. Maybe he'd go with her to the police, help give her some credibility. She's a journalist, for god's sake, trained to observe and report. Well, a soon-to-be graduate, but still… An employee at the local newspaper. A trustworthy source. Then it would all be in the hands of the police.

Today was a Monday, last day of the month. She'd go to the office first to see if she could find Mr. Martineau. If not, well, she could call in a report to the police, or go see them, or go see Martineau on Tuesday, or go see Martineau and the police on Tuesday.

Hell.

Maybe she didn't have to hurry so much. She couldn't identify the shooter anyway and the dead man was certainly not going anywhere. She didn't have to figure it out all at once. She should just take it one step at a time.

What a horrible thing to witness.

She looked back along the faint bike trail, her tire tracks visible in the dust. She missed her Saturday afternoons at the mall, footsteps against the terrazzo, the parade of people in bunny slippers, motorcycle helmets, you name it. The little shop that sells her favorite fingernail polish. What made her think of all these things, just now?

Her mind refocused on the man encased

in concrete.

Then an ache in her chest opened, an aperture widening at the edges, a cold darkness inside. The loss of her mother to Covid had been sudden, its transmission an isolated event that had cheated them both of so much life. Years of sharing and support swept away by an errant cough, a deviant without a mask, a so-called adult without the proper respect for others. She still couldn't accept the stupidity of it. Or the brutishness. And she couldn't dwell on it without tearing up, without the emotion of it seizing her breath. Though a bit less frequent now, these moments of sadness and dread still chained her to a leaden weight, ever ready to drag her into a deep, black hole.

She looked along the trail again and tried to clear her head. The path angled higher to her left, away from the edge of the cliff. She stood, re-shouldered her small pack, and turned her bike around. If she remembered correctly, the main trail was back toward the upper lip of the plateau, maybe a half-mile away.

She could still get back to the newspaper office by late afternoon.

CHAPTER 8

Relic marveled at the swirling smells – meatloaf, ketchup, carrots, buttered potatoes, coffee, blueberry pie, all laid out in a smorgasbord from heaven. Angels in smocks and hairnets stood behind plexi-glass shields, smiling, nodding at hot trays of food in front of them, scooping and plopping it onto your plate even if you didn't ask for it.

He followed Manny along the line, taking his cues from those around him. Voices carried over each other, cross currents in English and Spanish, urgent but happy, a communal meal among men with calloused hands, strong backs, sunburned necks.

He pointed to the berry pie and a plate of it slid onto his tray. They moved to a dispenser with ice water. Relic filled his glass and downed it without taking a breath. He refilled it and hurried to a seat next to Manny.

"Great food," Manny mumbled, a third of his plate

already empty.

Relic nodded as he ate.

Twenty men crowded along tables set up in the narrow trailer, bumping elbows, shoveling food, joking with each other, getting back in line for more.

"Looks like some Pueblo guys at the far table," Relic mumbled through his food.

"*Sí*. A lot of workers from the Indian reservations around here."

Baskets of dinner rolls were placed along the tables. Relic took one, made sure no one was looking, and tucked it into a side pocket on his cargo pants. He waited a moment, then took two more.

Relic's stomach filled quickly. But maybe he could stuff another bite of pie in there...

A man in a white dress shirt entered the room and stood in the doorway. The voices lowered a few decibels, workers reacting to his arrival, but after a moment, the talk relaxed again, returning to its original chaos.

"Who's he?" Relic leaned closer to Manny.

"Big boss. Manages the hotel and the whole project. Mr. Burke."

"So the big guy back at the water tower – he works for Burke?

"*Sí.*"

"The big guy is some kind of security here, eh?"

"*Sí*. There are at least two of them. Big *hombres*, some have been seen with pistols." Manny gave him a meaningful look. "Do not mess with them and they will leave you alone."

"Got it. You don't usually see that kind of security on a construction site, do you?"

"No."

The man in the doorway turned and left the building.

"Are the security men all *gringos?*"

"*Sí*." Manny looked at Relic from under his brow. "What are you thinking?"

He'd keep his promise to Manny this afternoon and see what else he could learn. And he'd need to collect some drinking water for his pack. "*Nada*, my friend. Just watching."

Manny nodded cautiously, a disbeliever.

Relic reached for another dinner roll.

CHAPTER 9

Hailey returned the bike and gear to Dean's Cycle Emporium and walked to a bench along the street. Her forearms and thighs felt liquefied, her fingers slow to move. From exhaustion or nerves, or both, her head seemed to float like a soap bubble, fragile and empty. She plopped onto the outdoor pew.

Tourists meandered the sidewalks in indecisive loops, looking into store windows, rocking on their heels, pocketing their hands, a casual afternoon visit. A gaggle of grade-school children ran gleefully through a herd of slow-moving adults, weaving through them with playful purpose. The sights and sounds were so radically different from the murder she'd seen that the memory of it felt strangely distant, as remote as the lonely bike trail she'd used that morning. But when she focused on it, the violence was like a screaming explanation point, a red-hot arrow pointing to the gun, the man's fall, the tomb of cement.

The newspaper office was down the street a couple of blocks, so she'd best get on with it, see if her editor was there. He was an important man in town, well known and, she assumed, well respected. He would know what to do; he would help her navigate this crisis.

She rose from the bench, her bones feeling a little more reliable. She took her time, keeping her breathing calm and regular. She was not looking forward to telling anyone what she'd seen. A woman in tight jeans and a bright blue shirt watched her intently then pulled her gaze to the sidewalk. Hailey realized that she must look like a wreck – sweaty, dusty, scraped-up, disheveled. No makeup whatsoever. Great way for her boss to see her, she thought, before even her first day on the job.

The newspaper had a modest storefront, "Red Rock Sentinel" stenciled in yellow on the glass. The serifs were randomly chipped, the letter "o" missing entirely. The door swung open suddenly, the little bell above it heralding someone's exit and she stopped. Two men were leaving the building.

"Sorry to get us so late to the greens today."

"It doesn't change our wager, you know."

"Mr. Martineau?" She stepped forward and her boss turned toward her.

"Hailey?"

Her editor's rounded belly seemed to boast of its own abundance, his jowls soft and loose. With a longer beard, the man could have played Santa Claus at Christmas, but his eyes were too small for his head, dark pebbles in a sandy face – intelligent, but with little warmth or humor.

The other man wore slacks and a light jacket, his back to her.

"Mr. Martineau, do you have a moment?"

"We're on our way to the club, but Bruce…" her boss turned toward the other man. "I'd like you to meet our new intern."

Bruce spun on his heel and faced her. He wore a black polo shirt with the words "Broken Inn" embroidered in red above the pocket.

"Hailey, this is Bruce Burke, manager of the soon-to-be reopened Broken Inn."

His head was narrow and long, his features a little angular. Parentheses framed his mouth as if an artist had sketched extra lines on the man's face, just for practice. His expression seemed to be a rehearsed kind of bland, a neutral façade, but the sight of him stopped the blood flow in her brain.

She couldn't tell whether he was the man who'd

murdered someone at the old inn this morning.

"Good afternoon." Burke nodded at Hailey and slid a pair of mirrored sunglasses onto his face, the kind she hated. You could never tell when someone was looking at you behind those praying mantis eyes.

Her editor stepped back and crossed his arms, examining her. "You know, Hailey, you need to do an article on the reopening of the old inn, an introduction or a re-introduction to the place."

Burke stood still as a statue.

She managed to inhale a little oxygen.

"You should focus," Martineau continued, "on Mr. Burke here, his plans, the new addition. His business is bringing much needed jobs to our county – construction work at first, then good jobs in the hospitality sector. He's joined the chamber of commerce and sits on the governor's business development task force, you know. Focus on the many positive aspects of this great project. Maybe even two articles, one on the here and now, one on the history of the old place, or weave the two together." The editor stopped, waiting for a reaction from her.

"Yeah, yeah." She shuffled her feet against the sidewalk. "Of course."

"Good. See Ash in the morning, eight o'clock sharp. He's our photographer, part-time anyway, but he'll show you your workspace and help you get started. Get out to the inn by, say…" he rose his brow at Burke.

"Nine is good."

"…nine in the morning. Interview Mr. Burke, look around the place, tell Ash what you want photographs of, and he'll go out there later. Your first assignment!" Martineau raised and lowered his hand, a chop in the air, an end to the directive.

Hailey nodded.

"Let's get going, Bruce. Loser buys supper." He moved past Hailey and down the sidewalk.

"Nice to meet you," Burke's lips narrowed into something pencil-thin when he smiled, an expression she found profoundly unsettling.

CHAPTER 10

Relic wiped the sweat from his forehead with the back of his hand, the leather glove rough against his skin. He rested his hands on his hips and took a breath. He'd lifted and carried dozens of cinder blocks from a semi-truck parked near the new foundation and lined them up along the outer wall, about a hundred feet long. Masons applied their mortar and placed each block along a concrete foundation, north side to south. They'd moved back to the beginning and laid a second row atop the first. He was used to hard work, but not to hauling thirty-five pounds in each hand, every three minutes.

The bourgeoning wall was long enough for three big trucks to pull in, and he wondered if that was its purpose or whether it would be sub-divided later for something smaller. He didn't pretend to know how a hotel would be constructed, but most of the addition seemed to be for storage. The northern wall was still low but with wide openings, maybe to house large, overhead doors. The eastern and western walls were taking shape, each allowing for one regular-sized door a piece.

The desert sun lay close to the canyon rim, stretching shadows across the ground. Manny labored up the slope to the semi-truck there and said something to the others, waving them toward him. The masons stopped their work and stood, stretching their muscles. Manny moved behind the long truck and spoke to the men as they walked past him, a nod, a friendly hello as they headed for the trailers below.

A dog walked from behind the new wall and sat in front of Relic, staring at him, some kind of canine mind-melding exercise. Thin and dusty, the dog seemed to be a combination of border collie and coyote, a mongrel whose pointed ears flopped just a little on the ends. Relic pulled the gloves from his hands. He plucked a dinner roll from his pocket and tossed it to the mutt, who continued to stare for a moment then casually took the meal from the ground and trotted off. He was hungry, but he wasn't begging.

Relic strode toward Manny when the semi-truck suddenly began to roll backward, toward a dip in the ground, straight for Manny's back.

"Watch it!" Relic sprinted toward the moving truck.

Manny turned to face Relic, a question in his eyes. "Truck!" Relic pointed.

Manny seemed confused for a moment then turned to see the semi rolling toward him. He stepped away from the truck just as it lurched into the spot he'd been standing.

Relic skidded to a stop in the dust.

"Oh!" The driver set the brake and the tires slid to a halt. "Sorry about that. Is everyone OK?"

Manny's eyes went to the truck bed, inches from his head. He looked back to Relic. "¡Caramba!"

"Gotta watch yourself." Relic spread his arms.

"¡A Dios mio! Gracias, my friend! I am tired and did not notice it." He shook his head.

The truck driver looked at them, concern in his eyes. "Sorry. I didn't think she'd roll." He'd put in the clutch to start the truck without setting the brake.

Relic waved dismissively. No harm, no foul. The driver slid back inside the cab and closed the door. The engine coughed a surge of dark smoke into the air and revved as the clutch engaged. The semi moved slowly down the road toward the river, relieved of its load of cinder blocks.

"I think I owe you another meal. Join us?" Manny pointed toward the trailers down by the river.

"Not again today, thank you. But I need water for my pack."

"Where is your pack?"

"Higher up, above the building and the water tower. Close to the spring."

Manny thought for a moment. "I know. Stay here. You are tired. Sit by the wall for a bit. If anyone asks, tell them you are waiting for me to pick you up."

Relic nodded. He moved to the low wall and sat in the dirt, resting his back against the fresh-laid blocks. Manny walked down the road, toward the trailers. Other workers strode from the site, one or two or three at a time, tired, moving slowly toward the dining hall he'd been in today at lunch.

A sleepy sun lowered itself to bed along the distant plateau, haze spreading from the flames, an ethereal comforter.

He rested for what felt like a long time, pondering the project he'd worked on that afternoon. Maybe those two guys he'd saved from the flash flood had been scouting the whole area. But what made anyone think the old inn could be a success? After two failed attempts over the years, why should people come to this hotel now?

An old Dodge pickup, its paint a faded green, rose along the road and stopped near the corner of the foundation. Manny hopped out and Relic stood.

"Here." He handed Relic a set of keys. "Take this up to the spring and leave it there. Just leave the keys in the ignition and someone will get it later."

"The truck?"

"I've put food and water on the front seat for you."

Relic opened the door. The smell of fresh chicken filled the cab. Two foil-wrapped plates rested on the seat. A heavy, plastic jug, the kind used in office water coolers, sat on the floor. He noticed two baggies between the plates, one of peanuts and one of round, chocolate candies. Peanut M&Ms, he thought, separated like twins at birth.

"Gracias," Relic smiled.

"There's a couple spare bunks in the trailers, if you need a place to sleep tonight."

"No, but thank you again."

"Come back to work tomorrow if you want to join us. We will gladly keep feeding you. Could even pay you if you stick around."

"You're a kind and generous man." Relic dipped his head, a nod of respect.

"Stay out of trouble, hombre."

"I'll do only what I can."

CHAPTER 11

Hailey stood on the sidewalk, staring at the faded "Red Rock Sentinel" letters and the offices inside, all dark and locked away for the night. She tried to rouse herself from what had just happened.

What *had* just happened?

Had Burke been the man in the white shirt, the one who'd fired a bullet into another man's head? Was he the man who'd spun his arm in the air, commanding the workers to leave, ordering another man to pour concrete on the dead man's grave? Could someone really do that and then go play a round of golf? Or did he know anything about it at all?

Shit.

She walked north along the street toward another public bench, but just as she moved closer, a man and woman slid onto the seat. Pushed aside, she thought. That figures. She put her hands in her pockets and kept moving away from the center of the small town, wandering.

She needed to report the crime to the police. But what proof did she have? She should have used her cellphone camera up there on the bike trail, taken some pictures. But, no, she was too far away for that. She'd seen what she'd seen through her binoculars. She did see it, didn't she? Had her eyes played a trick on her? Was there another explanation for what had happened?

Her boss was friends with the manager of the old inn. Would she – should she – bother him about something that might be a mistake? Accuse a man who sat on the governor's task force, or whatever it was? Would the sheriff be friends with Burke, too? Would he believe an outsider like her if she reported the crime? She couldn't afford to lose this job. But she had to do something.

Think.

Maybe her first assignment could be useful. She had to interview Burke tomorrow morning. She could start with the usual questions but probe a little, too – get Burke to agree to let her walk through the site. She could find the corner foundation where the murder occurred, maybe snap a couple of pictures with her phone, ask when the concrete had been poured, confirm that it had been done this morning.

Then, go to the sheriff.

That sounded right – get some corroborating facts first. She should confirm as much as she could before she took it all to the sheriff. She could talk to the police tomorrow afternoon.

If she didn't lose her nerve.

CHAPTER 12

Monday evening had passed well, Relic taking the time to refill his water bladder and bottles with the "office cooler" water Manny had provided. And he'd eaten well, too: roasted chicken, baked potatoes, green beans. After supper, he'd hiked along the plateau, just upstream from the old inn. The plastic jug Manny had given him still had plenty of water in it, so he'd cached it by a natural shelter above the rim.

Now it was early Tuesday morning, so he knew the workers would soon be back on the job. He hiked to a spot a couple hundred yards above the spring. The faded green pickup truck was gone – as Manny had said, someone must have collected and returned it.

Sakwa Spring had begun to replenish its supply of water overnight, but the water line was still far too low. The spring had been an oasis for thousands of years, a place several tribes shared throughout history. It was a place to be honored and respected, a place to be appreciated. And these fools, these jackasses, had nearly drained her entirely, endangering all the life that depends on it — tadpoles, insects, spiders, crows, coyotes.

He kneeled behind a rock and scanned the area. The man he'd seen yesterday, the giant with the bulbous nose, stood over an engine by the pump. A dark blue pickup truck sat parked behind him. The man pulled on something again, and again, and the sound of a motor reached Relic's ears. The giant had replaced the engine on the pump.

Relic waited.

The man walked over to the spring. Satisfied that the new pump was sucking the life from it, he looked about and returned to his truck. The giant drove away, a tail of dust swirling in his wake.

Relic took his time walking down to the spring, letting the giant put some distance between them. He reached the new engine, a little larger than the first, its beating piston jarring the air. A large hose shivered on the ground as water surged inside, a dead rubber tube animated by the movement of life-giving liquid.

He removed the air filter, gathered a cup of fine, red dust in the palm of his hand, and poured it slowly into the carburetor, choking the engine to a stuttered end.

He replaced the filter, brushed his hands on his pants, and set off toward the old part of the inn, the section not under active construction.

The sounds of clanking metal, straining engines, and whirling saws spread across the canyon, men at work on the other end of the project. The original inn was two stories high and faced the Colorado River. The back side stretched for several yards to a wall that angled ninety degrees away for about twelve feet and resumed its parallel path with that side of the inn. It seemed like this part would have been an addition to the hotel, but the original roof line showed that it was part of the design, maybe some sort of back hall access for the hotel staff. A door at the end of it faced away from the new construction, hidden from the activity on the north side of the project. He skidded down a slope behind the hotel and trotted to the door.

"More…and water for the concrete mixer…"

Voices seemed to be moving toward him, along the outside of the back access, coming from the new addition. He twisted the old doorknob.

Locked.

"…Well, somebody's gonna get shit-canned for that…"

Relic turned the handle as far as he could and

tugged up, then down, stressing the natural give in the aging lock.

"…check with Burke…"

He strained against the tired hardware, pulling, twisting, hanging his weight against it.

"…don't know…"

The voices were nearly around the corner.

The latch slipped with a muffled click. He opened the door, slid quickly inside, and held it closed against the frame. The men were suddenly past the corner, the sound of their boots distinct. They stopped for a moment. One of them turned the knob but Relic held it tightly, leaning his weight into it, as if it were secured.

After two quick tries, the men outside seemed satisfied and they resumed their walk along the building.

Relic turned and let his eyes adjust to the darkness. Sunlight filtered through cracks in the roof and wall. A hallway ran a few feet in front of him to an inside door whose frame angled to the left – a large storage room, perhaps. He walked carefully over the old floor, its surface worn and warped, its bones creaking at every step. He reached the door and slowly turned the handle. At first it seemed to be locked, but like the outside door, a stern wiggle back and forth freed the latch.

The hinges squealed an objection and there was no

artificial light inside. No one seemed to be in the room.

Strips of wide plastic hung from the ceiling to the floor like a film. Behind them hung elongated shapes resembling emaciated people, their heads hung onto their chests. He took a breath and pulled back the curtain.

A row of yellow, rubberized suits dangled in front of him, helmets attached to their collars, the universal symbol for hazardous material stenciled on their chests.

CHAPTER 13

Hailey balanced a tray of coffees as she pulled open the door to the Red Rock Sentinel. She spun inside, adjusted the purse on her shoulder, and let the door hiss closed behind her. She'd barely slept, worrying about what she'd seen at the old inn, second guessing herself, settling down, then questioning herself again. In the end, she'd finally relinquished, settling on her plan. She'd fallen asleep as the sun began to rise.

A long counter blocked public access. Two metal chairs sat near a green, sun-bleached newspaper box, the kind found on streets and porticos for the sale of newspapers. Four metal desks were arrayed behind the counter and, behind them, an office with "E. Martineau, Editor" painted on frosted glass in the door. A waist-high door rested on spring-loaded hinges at the end of the counter, access to the offices behind the public space. To her right, a store front window faced the street. Dust motes floated under the glare of the glass and the building smelled of antiques and leather, an old west museum on a shoestring budget.

"Hello?" A male voice came from someplace out of view.

"Hello," she replied.

A man in his early twenties strode out between the desks, hair dark and longish, curls bouncing against his shirt collar. He held an expensive looking camera against his chest, its weight anchored around his neck.

"Can I help you?" A pair of gray-blue eyes gave her a friendly once-over.

She cleared her throat. "I'm Hailey."

"Of course, that's what I thought. No customers are ever here this early." He glanced at the tray of cups.

"Oh, I thought I'd bring fresh coffees. Two of them are salted caramel macchiato with whipped cream."

"From Jaimie's, the place on the corner?"

"Yeah." She carried the cardboard platter with one hand.

"Best place in town. I'm Ash, by the way." He walked toward the swinging door at the far end of the counter.

She moved quickly to the door and shoved it open, but it struck his leg hard and bounced back against her thighs, jarring the coffee forward, the tray tipping downward, too fast for her to correct, two cups lurching forward to an awful collision, a seismic splash-down all over his jeans.

"Oh, oh that's hot." He jumped back, raising his camera with one hand, brushing his crotch with the other.

"Oh my god, I'm so sorry." She placed the other two cups on the counter. "Let me…"

"No, it's hot but I'm OK." He turned away from her, shaking one leg, then the other.

She steadied her hands on the swinging door. One hell of a way to start a job. "I'm so sorry, I'm such a klutz this morning."

"Really, I'll live." He turned back to her. "But I will need to go home and change."

"Oh…" His pants were soaked. "Is the camera OK?"

"Yeah, it's all below the waistline."

She cringed.

"Tell you what…" Ash placed the camera on one of the desks. "Why don't you check out your station," he pointed to another desk behind him. "Fire up the computer, the code is just redrocknews, and get familiar with it. I'll be back in a bit."

"I've got an interview at nine, out at the Broken Inn." She couldn't look him in the eye.

"Oh, well, you'd better do that first. It'll take you thirty or forty minutes to get there."

"Yeah, I think I'd better do that, before I do any more damage here." She tried to smile.

"It's OK. Hey, leave one of those for me." He pointed to the coffees on the counter.

She pulled one out of its cardboard carrier. "I'll take this one for the road."

"Martineau doesn't usually come in 'till noon, but if I see him first, I'll tell him you were here."

"If he hasn't fired me by then," she said under her breath.

CHAPTER 14

"Shit on a shingle." Relic ran his hand over one of the hazmat suits. Everything else in this old inn was rusty or dusty, but these rain-slickers seemed nearly new. A pair of clean, rubber boots stood dutifully at the feet of each hanging suit. What the hell were they doing here?

He dropped the curtains, closed the door, and backed away. The hallway stretched to his right, so he moved cautiously in that direction. A row of bare light-bulbs hung along the center of the ceiling, power off, but sunlight filtered through slits in the wall, places where siding had slipped and cracked open over time. He came to another inside door and it opened easily, revealing a hallway into the old inn, probably leading to the main hall used by guests. He passed two more similar doorways on his left and noticed light streaming from beneath slits in the floorboards up ahead. He walked quietly to the light and kneeled to look.

Though illumination spread from beneath, he could not see into the space below. But it seemed there was a basement under this part of the old inn – the light was artificial. The space was being used.

He stood and moved farther down the hall until he reached another door leading to the outside. He pressed his ear to the wood.

The grunts and scattered words of a team of men filtered through the door. He was on the north side of the old inn now, right next to the addition being built, the area he'd carried cinder blocks to the previous afternoon. Manny had said there were usually two security guards, including the giant he'd encountered the day before. At least one of them had likely gone past him at the other end of this structure, when he'd ducked inside. He'd have to keep a close look out for the other one.

He opened the door a couple of inches and peered out, the sounds of a busy workplace now flooding over him. The exit was a couple of feet above ground level.

He moved quickly out the door and balanced on a stone that was part of the old foundation. He closed the door behind him. A stack of two-by-fours lay to his right. One worker carried a load on this shoulder toward the opposite end of the addition. Relic jumped to the ground and went to the wood. He lifted several of the boards onto his shoulder and followed the other man.

They'd poured several new sections of concrete since he'd last seen it, roped off to keep people away until it hardened. The man in front of him dropped his load of wood and turned for more. He nodded at Relic as he passed, an unspoken thanks for the help. Relic rolled the two-by-fours off his shoulder into the same stack and looked around. He noticed a shovel leaned against some cinder blocks, went to it, and hoisted it onto his shoulder – a farmer out to clear the ditches. He moved to the edge of the activity, north of the addition.

An eighteen-wheeler truck rumbled up the road from the north, heading toward the site, its load hidden by canvas tarps. But instead of turning into the project, the truck continued along the road, past the old inn, south toward Demon's Roost, the place he'd saved those men from the flash flood a few weeks ago. Why would the truck go past the construction site?

He stared at the project a while, sensing its rhythm, men moving to and from the site, trucks driving in what seemed like random intervals, walls growing slowly, steadily higher. A white and orange backhoe was parked a few yards away. A yellow bulldozer rested on the dirt road in front of the old inn. He could see the narrow trailers sitting parallel to each other down the slope, the temporary mess hall and housing for the workers. Trucks and cars were parked along the road near the trailers, transportation for the employees.

One of the security guards he'd seen yesterday emerged from behind the cinder block wall, maybe twenty yards away, his head swiveling round, watching the men. His eyes seemed to catch on Relic.

It was time to move along.

CHAPTER 15

Hailey didn't know whether she could drive directly to the inn itself, where she was to meet with Mr. Burke, so she pulled her old Blazer into an open spot along the dirt road near a row of three trailers and a bunch of other vehicles. She hopped out, straightened her blue oxford shirt, and dusted off her pants. She walked along the lane, past the mobile homes, and up an incline to the front entrance of the inn. A new porte cochère shaded the entrance. Fresh walls, covered in weatherproof sheathing, stretched from the corner of the building to about thirty yards down, where the old structure resumed. Maybe they were renovating one section at a time.

She'd woken several times during the night, imagining worse to come – Burke being the killer, telling her he'd seen her watching, threatening her, inviting her to a swim in some cement. She rejected those chilling thoughts, reminding herself that Burke had already met her and said nothing, that he didn't look like a murdering fiend, that she was just obsessing about it all. She wanted badly to ask him about the killing but remembered her resolve to see the sheriff after the interview. So, she'd listed her questions on a steno pad she kept by her bed for jotting down random thoughts. She would keep her focus narrow, businesslike.

After spilling coffee on the photographer, she'd nearly gone home and back to bed.

She squared her shoulders and opened the door. Inside, glossy drawings of the finished project were hung on her right. A marble hotel countertop stretched along her left, smooth but chalky. A half-built fireplace sat directly ahead, rough stones stacked alongside to become its façade.

"Hailey."

She jumped a little at the sound of Burke's voice.

He stepped into the foyer and shook her hand. "Good to see you this morning."

"Good morning."

"Come back to my office."

She followed him into a spacious room, its walls painted a pale blue, its plywood floor unadorned. An empty bookshelf rested on the far side, a citizen's band radio set on top.

"We're working to get a cell phone tower, but until then," Burke waved toward the radio, "that lets us talk with the incoming truckers." He sat behind a heavy wooden desk and pointed to a chair in front of him. "I'd offer you coffee, but I see you have some."

"Yes, thanks anyway."

"Carpeting comes later." He pointed to the bare floor.

"Sure."

He asked where she was from, where she'd gone to college, whether she was glad to be working with Mr. Martineau. Pleasantries completed, she asked him about the size of the project, its budget, the number of construction workers and how many hotel employees it would eventually support. They had on-site security – Odin, the really big guy, and Mason. He recited the information from memory, enjoying the opportunity to display his mastery of the subject and all its positive aspects. What about water? Electricity? Plumbing? He had easy answers for all of them.

Hailey checked her notes. "The original inn was built in the 1950s and was renovated in the 1970s, then closed down again. If you don't mind me asking, why do you think it will succeed this time?"

"After the end of the Covid-19 crisis, tourism is at

an all-time high. The population in this area is growing like a weed, and this county is short on hotel space. Plus, what we'll offer here is right along the river. Whitewater rafting, horseback riding, we're even planning a small ghost town with weekend entertainment. We've studied the potential, of course, and our bankers had to be satisfied, too. The jobs and tax revenue will be substantial, something your boss appreciates."

After nearly thirty minutes, she found herself flummoxed. Did she really think she could tell if someone was a murderer just by looking at them? Or listening to them? She checked her notes and shook her head. This interview was not helping.

Burke's lips and nose were thin, neat lines on either side. His eyes were brown, crow's feet tugged along the edges, a man still young but showing signs of strain. She realized she might be staring and moved her eyes to her steno pad, trying to focus on her scribbles there. She needed to ask about the concrete – when was it poured, when would it set up? She rubbed her left hand across her pants, drying a bit of sweat.

His cell phone buzzed. He lifted a finger, a signal to wait a moment, and took the call.

She'd listened closely to his answers, searching for any signs of dishonesty or cruelty. She had nothing.

"Say, Hailey, I've got to talk with my construction manager." Burke slid his phone into his pocket. "Why don't you look around and call me if you have any more questions. Just be careful not to go into the old part of the inn. There are still parts of it that my carpenters tell me are not safe – it's over sixty years old in places."

"Oh." Part of her told her to raise the subject now, to be that pressing, investigative reporter, but she hesitated, unsure at the last second, letting the opportunity pass. She closed her writing pad and tucked it into her purse.

"Nice to meet you." He offered his hand and she shook it, kicking herself for backing away from her task. "Follow me this way." He led her out of the office, through the foyer and outside the building.

"OK, then, I'm sure we'll talk again sometime. Tell your boss I said you're doing a great job."

"Thank you." She reminded herself that many famous killers had been charming.

She watched him hurry across the road and down toward the mobile trailers. He was quickly out of sight.

She took a deep breath; the meeting was over and she hadn't even asked about any injuries on the work site. She turned and looked behind her, into the unfinished lobby of the hotel. Adjacent to the central fireplace was a large room and a hallway, presumably leading to the hotel rooms. She glanced back outside. No one was paying any attention to her. Maybe there was a better way to get some solid information.

Hailey ducked into the lobby and wandered down the hall. A wooden door appeared on her left and she tried the handle.

Open.

Stairs led down into what might be a basement to the inn. She noticed light seeping from another door lower down, but no one seemed to be around. Burke had told her to check the project. It was not clear to her whether this was part of the old hotel or the part that had been renovated, the part it was all right to explore. She'd feel better about her hesitation earlier if she could gather some information now, something to give the sheriff more than her uncorroborated story about a man buried in concrete.

She walked purposefully down the stairs and toward the light from under the door. She approached it slowly, listening for sounds from within. The place was graveyard quiet. A hallway with stone walls led into the dark to her left, toward the northern end of the building. Probably the original foundation. She refocused on the door and turned the knob. Though it seemed very old, it must have been oiled – it made no noise when she pulled it open. She stepped inside and closed it behind her.

The room was longer than it was wide and seemed to lead to other rooms, dark, rectangular entries to hidden spaces, filled with dust and mold. A work bench anchored the stone wall on her left, more of the original foundation. She stepped to the work area, wrenches, screwdrivers, and screws scattered across the top, not dusty at all. Beyond that was some kind of metal box with a gauge on the front, a clear, square shape with a red needle inside. A tool for measuring something.

She walked farther into the room, running her fingers along the edge of the work bench until she came to three weird items she could not identify. Each had a centerpiece of sorts, glass or plastic rectangles above their centers, narrow, like the cockpit windows on a commercial airplane. Canisters of some sort were attached to the sides of each, protruding outward, holes on the ends of them. Masks, she realized. Like the ones used to protect someone from tear gas.

She touched the closest one.

"Hey!"

A man the size of goliath stood in a darkened doorway twenty feet away from her.

"Hey, get over here!" He pushed his hands together, flexing his biceps and when he stepped toward her, an electric jolt ran through her brain, all instinct screaming at her to run, to get away from this monster of a man as fast as she possibly could, and she spun and sprinted for the door.

CHAPTER 16

She sped through the opening, but as soon as she passed the stairway, she realized her mistake, and it was too late – she couldn't go back the way she'd come. She touched a corner of the old stone wall as she spun past, propelling into the dark hallway like a rat fleeing a lion, taking the only choices presented and taking them as fast as she could.

"Get back here!"

The man's voice was as huge as his chest, the sound of a wrestler who could crush her windpipe with a single hand. She ran hard into the black for twenty yards or more, stumbling over debris along the floor but staying on her feet. The dark closed ever more tightly around her, icy as winter asphalt.

She quickly became but a ghost in the depths, weightless and lost, passing through space as black and pitch as solid rock. She slowed to a cautious shuffle.

A deep echo reached her ears, footfalls long and methodical.

She pulled her purse behind her and stretched both arms forward, feeling through the ether. She touched a sudden hardness on her right, startling her. She slid her hand lightly along the rough surface as she walked. How deep did this hallway go?

"Hey!" The voice was frustrated now. The dark was slowing his progress, too.

The wall seemed to bend to her left. She kept her right hand on the stone foundation, waving her other hand in front of her face in case she came quickly to another wall, or, god forbid, the end of the structure. Each step became painful, the expectation of another barrier, the raw surprise it would present, the uncertainty of it all. She struggled to put one foot in front of the other, pressing forward for what seemed like a very long distance but could only have been a few yards.

Slowly, ever so faintly, something seemed to be tickling the back of her retina. Was it her imagination? She closed her eyes, turned her head, and opened them again. The tiny change was off to her left. She stepped a little faster now and a particle of hope began to pulse through her – the discovery of light up ahead. She increased her pace, no longer fearful of running headlong into a wall. The light brightened as she approached, bluish photons bouncing through tiny fissures in the mortar.

She heard the scrape of shoes on dirt behind her then a stumble, a hard fall, and a brutal curse.

Quickly, she groped toward the leaking light and began tugging at the sandstone blocks. She chose the nearest one, pulling, yanking, scraping her hands across it, wiggling it to the left, the right, the left, then pushing hard, leaning her weight into it. The rock finally began grinding forward, away from her, sliding against the stone below, and suddenly fell free, out into the open.

She could smell fresh air.

Footfalls behind her resumed their pace.

She reached for another block, pressing it sideways, shoving, grunting, pushing until it spun from its place in the wall and tumbled outside. Light now filled the dark tunnel, spotlighting her.

Footfalls behind her gathered speed.

She dived through the narrow space, too soon, she realized, too small for her to fit, so she pushed another stone with her elbow, working it back and forth, back and forth, finally past her head, and she was bumbling forward, falling with the stone, swimming into sand and rocky debris on the other side, scratching her face, scraping her arms, almost there, almost there...

Her purse jammed hard against a jagged spot in the wall and stopped her cold.

CHAPTER 17

Hailey slipped her shoulder from the purse's strap and slid into a rough ditch, past the basement wall. She grabbed the purse, snatching it from the stones, and this time placed the leather braid over both her head and her shoulder.

"Get back here!"

The man had reached the wall, his arm stretched into the air beyond it, groping for her. He pulled himself back inside and began removing rocks from the wall, just as she had done.

She turned and stumbled forward along a ditch that ran steeply upward toward the level surface. The sounds of men at work filled the air. She struggled up the slope, feet slipping, twisting, pushing her forward until she reached the top. She took a quick breath and glanced about.

Suddenly, the giant was upon her, grabbing her

shoe, his fingers squeezing against her heel.

"No!" She spun and crunched her other foot into his hand and he cursed and released his grip. He slid back down the ditch but soon was climbing up again, crawling on his hands and feet.

She thought to scream, but why would the workers help her? The giant was probably a security guard for the project. The workers might even come to his aid.

She ran away, a straight line toward a yawning canyon, not daring to look back. She found her pace, keeping it fast but steady across the hardened ground. Ahead, the cliffs opened like a standing book, rising quickly on either side of her. The ground became uneven, a challenge in her hard-soled flats. She dodged loose rocks, cacti, and tufts of desert grass. A narrow trail appeared before her, snaking its way on a steeper incline into the canyon.

Hailey re-doubled her pace along the path, working her lungs like a bellows, concentrating on just the space ahead of her, panic slowing to raw determination.

She glanced behind her.

The large man had slowed to a walk, his physique more suited to bench pressing than sprinting. She continued up the trail along a straight, sloping ridge, then around a boulder and into a series of short, steep switchbacks. She reached a chunk of sandstone the size of a small car and stopped to catch her breath. Below, she could see the man a half-mile away, trudging up the ridge. She'd put some nice distance between them, but he was dogged.

How far did this canyon go? Could she reach the top of the plateau and circle back into another canyon or into town? She wished she'd seen the sheriff first thing, before she'd come out here.

She pushed away from the rock and resumed a steady climb to a flattened area surrounded by a huge rock fall from the plateau above. She went quickly across the ground until the path twisted again into a set of switchbacks so steep that her feet slipped on the scree with every step. She tried to pace herself more slowly. If she could reach the top, maybe she could find a place to hide off-trail.

She rounded the knoll and stopped, leaning at the waist, hands on her knees, catching her breath again. She couldn't see the man below anymore, but when she turned back toward the trail, the gorge had narrowed dramatically to a pile of rock at the bottom and sheer cliffs above, four hundred feet all the way to the top.

She was at the foot of a box canyon with no good place to hide.

CHAPTER 18

She tried to slow her breathing when an unfamiliar voice reached her ears.

"Up here."

Her eyes scanned the brick-red cliffs, smooth as glass but for three vertical cracks, claw marks gouged by a mythical beast. One of them rose all the way to the top. Pedestals of stone split away from the northern side of the face, defiant chins jutting forward.

"Here…"

There he was, standing on a ledge halfway up the cliff, a man with a dark ponytail and pack waving for her to come toward him. What the hell? Why was he out here, directing her to follow?

She didn't know what to think. But, clearly, going back down was out of the question. She could hide, but the security guard had only to take his time walking around the rocks up here. She'd be found, for sure.

Damn it. The morning was turning into an utter disaster. She at least should have worn her cargo shorts and hiking boots.

She wound her way through boulders to the base of the cliff, where more fallen rock confronted her. She glanced at the man above to get her bearings and began to climb upward. When she reached a stone twelve feet high, she found a nearby rock to stand on and lifted herself, chin-up style, onto the slab. From there, a ledge made its crooked way higher up the wall. She glanced again at the man above, now only a few yards away.

She turned to see the guard reach the top of the knoll with the steep switchbacks. He had his head bent to the ground, breathing hard.

She swallowed; her throat was parched. The man with the ponytail was pointing the way up.

Great. Watch her get part way up the cliff and get stuck – no way up, no way down. But for now, at least, she could keep moving. Anything was better than waiting for the giant to crush her windpipe. She shifted to her right, stepping up a staircase of sorts, rocks jutting from the cliff in uneven elevations. So far, she'd not felt the height of her climb, but after reaching the end of these ledges, her head began to reel. She rested for a moment and watched the guard on the ground. He was looking all around him, circling the gorge methodically, but he was not looking up. He did not expect her to be on the face of the cliff.

Turning slowly again, she searched for the man with the ponytail. Now he seemed much closer, more level to her location. She could see a way to scoot along the ledge to reach him, but the edge was only about six inches wide. In places, the rock wall leaned outward and she would have to duck to stay even with the ledge to avoid leaning away from the cliff and falling off.

Shit.

She moved carefully forward, pressing her chest into the rock wall, keeping her head and purse to the side, eyes on the ground ahead of her. She glanced over the edge of the narrow path – a big mistake. The heights were right there, right below her feet, and made her head spin again. She focused on her discount leather shoes and tried to think about them instead – not great for trails, the soles a little too thin, but, still, they were flexible. They were sensible, she told herself, a reasonable choice. She slid one forward, then the next. Her torso was forced farther and farther out by the curve of the rock, leaning her weight behind her waist and she could feel the vertigo coming again, the loss of control. She lowered using her knees, allowing her to straighten at the waist again and lean back toward the cliff. Sweat trickled down her temples as she squatted and shuffled along.

Shortly, she was able to stand again and continued to the man waiting patiently there, encouraging her forward.

"Good job." He smiled broadly, a row of pearl white teeth in sharp contrast with his sun-darkened skin. "Now we have the tricky part."

She heaved each breath. "Tricky…part?"

"It's not bad. Here, take these." He handed her a pair of leather gloves. "I'll go first as a free climb, then tie in above and throw you the rope."

"Rope?"

"In my pack." He pointed behind him. "I'm going now. When you see the rope, tie it around your chest, under your arms. It's a safety measure, that's all."

Right. A safety measure. She craned her neck upwards, the cliff straight and smooth all the way to the sky, the top beyond her line of sight.

Hell.

She turned carefully to look below. The giant who'd been chasing her looked up, shielding his eyes from the sun. He'd seen them.

The man with the ponytail reached his fingers into a diagonal crack in the rock, pulled himself up, and put the toe of his boot on a rough spot nearby, flexing his knees. He sprung quickly upward, jamming his hand at a higher spot in the crack, pulling himself until his foot found a bulge on the sandstone face. She watched as he crawled vertically up the cliff face, grunting and straining as he went, higher and higher, his form smaller and smaller until it disappeared behind an outcrop.

She glanced below again. The guard was working his way up the loose scree, closer to the base of the cliff.

Feeling the crack with her fingers, she tried to imagine where to put her hands and feet for an ascent, but beyond about two yards, the cliff looked unclimbable. The man with the ponytail had made it look easy. Who the hell was he? *Where* the hell was he?

Stones clattered down the slope as the guard reached the rugged set of rocks she'd used as a stairway. She could see his face looking upward, sweating, and when his eyes reached hers, his lips curled in a joyless smile.

She pulled her gaze away and slapped her hands on her knees, anxiety ratcheting upward. The sound of rope sliding down the cliff drew her attention back to the wall. The climbing rope was dull and worn; something that would easily hold her weight when it was new. But how old was this thing? She wrapped it under her arms twice and tied it off in front. Had she used the right kind of knot?

Oh shit, oh shit, oh shit. Why had she left Seattle for some god-forsaken externship?

"Ready?" His voice seemed to spread out through the air. She still could not see him.

"Yes!"

"Climb!"

She slid her right hand into the crack in the rock and pulled herself up, stepping how she'd seen the man with the ponytail do it. She reached and stepped again, four feet above where she'd started. The rope gave a steady pull against her chest, helping her ascend.

The first several moves were not as difficult as she'd expected, but the rock became more polished higher up. She could not find a good toehold. She strained to pull her weight to the next level, her hands in the crack, her arms folded at the elbows, her face tight against the stone.

"Help," her voice squeaked, a plea to anyone, or no one.

She took her right hand from the crack and slid it higher, searching for another grip, holding her weight with one arm. Just as she looked upward, her left hand slipped out of the leather glove and she slammed against the cliff, sliding down, her forearms tearing across the pitiless rock, searing her skin. Suddenly, her momentum stopped, the rope fully tight against her shoulders. She put her right hand, the one still in a glove, onto the rope and hung there for a moment, panic threatening to loosen her nerve completely.

Remarkably, her body began rising upward, five or six inches at a time. The man was pulling her up. She tried to find some purchase with her feet, to no avail, but she slid her ungloved hand into the crack, lifting as much of her weight as she could. Soon, she was past the bald rock, rising to a one-inch ledge in the precipice where she grabbed hold and tugged, her breath heaving, sweat flowing freely from her forehead, her neck, her arms, everywhere, it seemed.

The cliff began to slope gently inward and she dared a glance up. The man with the ponytail strained mightily against the rope, pulling her with the force of his legs. Her weight seemed to lighten its grip a little, and she was able to get her feet underneath her hips and move to the open ledge where he was standing.

She slid to the ground, hugging it, gravity suddenly a security blanket wrapping her warmly to the spinning earth. She lay there for several moments.

"Made it." He stepped away from the edge.

"Yeah." She rolled onto her back and tried to sit up, her arms weak and shaky. She had to use both hands to scoot against a rock and catch her breath.

"I'll untie you." The man reached forward gently and worked the knot loose, then unwound it and slipped the rope from under her arms. He stepped back and wound it into a neat loop tied in the middle.

"I lost one of your gloves." She lifted her hands to show him.

"No worries." He pointed toward the cliff face. "It's slick as snot on a doorknob."

She handed him the remaining glove. He put it and the rope into his pack and sat cross-legged on the ledge.

"When you're ready, we can walk the rest of the way to the top." He cocked his thumb like a hitchhiker and pointed it behind him.

She nodded, still too tired to speak.

"No worries for now. That guy below can't follow us up here without climbing gear." He ran his fingers through a thin goatee, black as a crow's tail, and gazed into the canyon below.

Who the hell is this guy?

CHAPTER 19

Hailey had a hundred questions but, just as she opened her mouth, the man in the ponytail stood and motioned for her to follow. He trod steadily up an incline toward the top of the canyon wall.

She rose slowly from her seat, muscles protesting, pushing against the stone to help. She was going to ask where they were going, but the man was nearly out of earshot already. She leaned forward, letting her weight pull her into the final steps.

When she reached the top, her lungs were heaving again, so she stopped and rested her hands on her knees. Above the canyon walls, the world was suddenly open, huge, intimidating. She stood. The ground dipped gently ahead of them, freckled with tufts of pale grass and olive-colored sage as far as she could see. The sky seemed to swallow them here, its translucent blue beaming from horizon to horizon. She was on a distant planet, the edges visible in all directions. Nothing like the coastal rainforests.

The man was ahead of her, weaving among the brittle sage. There was no trail up here, so she followed his footprints in the sandy soil. After a while, her muscles seemed more limber, her breath less ragged, and she started to catch up with him. Or maybe he'd slowed his pace a bit.

They walked on and on, for miles it seemed. The sun lay low along the western rim, lighting a haze that made it all seem incredibly distant, each ridge more purple and remote than the last. In the eastern sky, clouds floated like cotton candy, pastels in shades of pink and blue.

Where the hell were they going? Were they going to get there by nightfall? Her muscles began to tighten again, her tongue dry as a cotton sock, her head throbbing.

They eventually reached a maw in the plateau, a place where Jurassic walls opened beneath them, hard-edged teeth drawing them down.

She hurried to follow him into the canyon.

The planet changed dramatically again here, the horizon quickly narrowing, shadows filling the gaps, cooling the air. They continued to weave along a solid bench of sandstone then dropped beneath it and onto a gentle slope.

"Here we are." He pointed to an overhang of rock. "Right in here…" He ducked his head and moved to the back of the cave-like formation.

"Here?" She whispered to herself. "Not back to the road? Not back to town?" She followed him in and found a place to sit. She rested her back against the stone wall, grateful for the reprieve.

He lowered his pack and removed two water bottles, one full, one empty. He tossed the full one to her. "I'm gonna refill this one before it's dark. Be back soon."

She nodded, too tired to object. She drank greedily from the bottle, stopped to catch her breath, and drank again. She pulled her knees to her chest and looked around. To her surprise, a low wall of brick-sized rock rose on her left, clearly man made. It was divided into two units, one body-size and empty, the other about three feet square, filled with things she could not identify – maybe a sack in there and something else with a handle. A fire ring rose against the empty enclosure, blocks of sandstone arranged into a neat semi-circle, black ash filling the center.

This was some kind of camp. Semi-permanent.

The sun dimmed quickly, draining the little canyon of its colors, cooling the air another notch or two.

She could barely see beyond the shelter anymore but heard his footsteps crunching against the gravel. He rounded the corner, arms loaded with twigs and branches, wood washed down from the plateau, she assumed. He dropped them by the fire pit and set the refilled water bottle nearby.

"One more load," he said, turning back into the growing darkness.

She huddled closer to the fire ring, anticipating some warmth.

After a while, he returned with another armload of wood and plants with slender stems, fuzzy cattails weighing on the ends. He set them on a flat rock nearby and set about arranging and lighting a fire. Then he rummaged through stuff within the wall of mortared rocks, his back to her.

"Ah-ha." He lifted a cooking pot with a small flair of discovery, a magician surprising his audience. She heard water pouring into the pot and he set it on the edge of the fire.

"Hungry?" A rising flame exaggerated his nose and goatee, sharp silhouettes in motion.

"Yeah." She scooted closer to the fire.

"Name's Relic. What's yours?"

Relic?

"I'm Hailey."

He placed the handful of stalks onto a flat rock and slid a hunting knife from a sheath on his belt. He sliced the root-like stems, the ones opposite the cattails, rinsed them with water, and tossed them into the pot.

"Cattails? Out here in the desert?"

"There's a little spring a few yards down."

"The cattails are for supper?" She wrinkled her nose.

He turned toward her, knife still in his hand, the tip shiny in the firelight. She swallowed.

"The hungrier you are, the better they taste."

"I'm sure that's true."

He moved the uncut plants to the side, tops bobbing like hotdogs on a stick. Sausages, she thought, would taste wonderful right about now.

"So, this looks like a pretty well-stocked camp for a hiker..."

He seemed to be looking for something else in his cache, ignoring her remark.

"Do you live out here?"

"Sometimes." He kept his back to her, still searching his gear.

"I have to thank you for that, for helping me back in that canyon. That was quick thinking with the rope."

"Ah..." He turned back to her, a squeeze bottle in

his hand. He nestled into a spot by the fire.

"Seriously. You live out here?"

"Seriously. Sometimes." His face at first displayed no emotion, no attitude at all, and then his lips parted into a playful smile, teeth straight and glossy.

She smiled at him and relaxed a beat.

"Why was that man chasing you?"

"Good question…I mean, I don't know what's going on there, but that man was huge and he started after me and I guess I panicked."

"You must've seen or heard something."

"Oh." A vision returned – concrete pouring over a fresh body. "I did. I guess that's what started it."

Relic canted his head, urging her to say more. The fire had settled into a steady burn, the view beyond their little shelter black as the tunnel she'd run through in her escape. The pot of water began to steam.

The murder that had started it all seemed so clear in her mind, but somehow in the distance, too, as if it had been weeks ago. "Yesterday, I went for a mountain bike ride, along some of the red rock trails."

Relic dropped cattail rhizomes into the pot.

"I stopped for a break and saw the old inn, the construction and all of that, so I got my binoculars and watched for a while. Wait – where's my purse?"

Relic pointed.

"Oh." She took a breath and pulled it close against her. For a moment, she thought she'd lost it.

"You took it off when we got here."

"Right, right. Well…" she hesitated a beat. "I saw something I wish I hadn't. There were guys at the corner of the new addition, laying a foundation. There was a concrete truck there. Then one guy went up to another and…"

Relic stroked his goatee.

"…shot him in the head," Hailey declared.

Relic pulled his hand from his face.

"He fell down into the place that was waiting for concrete, you know, and then, right there, they buried the dead guy with it. They even smoothed it out," she mimicked the action with her hands, "when they were done."

"Shit."

"Yeah!" She began to pat her hands against her knees. "And I looked and looked at it afterwards and you couldn't even tell they'd done anything at all, and they walked away like nothing happened and I even wondered once or twice if I'd really seen it, it was over so fast, you know?"

Relic gazed up at the walls of their little cave, worry in his eyes.

"So then, wait, that's not all, I went to my new boss, he's the editor of the Red Rock Sentinel, and who was there with him? The guy who runs the new inn, the man in charge of it all, they were running off to a game of golf, if you can believe it! Golf! I didn't know what to do…Then my boss says, go see the man – Burke's his name – and do a fluff piece on him for the paper so that's…"

"…slow down…"

"…what I did this morning, and he was cool as a cucumber, but when I looked around, I found the basement, like the original basement for the old inn and that huge guy with the bulging muscles saw me and chased me through a tunnel deep in the old foundation." She took a quick breath. "The place was pitch black, and I got away, just barely, and ran up the canyon…that's when I got ahead of him but then there was no way out of the canyon, until you helped me up and we got away and now I'm exhausted and hungry and scared and tired and wondering just what the hell is going on down there…"

She tried to slow her breathing. They sat quietly for a moment.

Relic lifted his knife and rubbed his thumb along the tip. "Something rotten has moved into the old inn."

CHAPTER 20

Mason waited under the porte cochère at the front of the inn, watching Odin approach. The man's head hung a little lower than usual, arms swinging with fatigue, the front of his shirt stained with dried sweat. Mason was chief of security for the renovation project, but he respected Odin as an equal. And even when Odin was tired, Mason couldn't help but respect the man's size and strength.

"Have anything to report?" Mason asked, knowing the man would.

"Yeah." Odin came to a stop. "I found a young woman in the basement, looking through some of our stuff down there, and she took off like a rabbit. Couldn't catch her." He shook his head.

"There's not much down there to see, is there?"

"No. But she ran, so I followed her all the way up to the end of that box canyon." He pointed his thumb behind him. "Weird thing is, when she had nowhere else to go, some guy threw her a rope, got her over the slick part of the rock and they both disappeared."

"Somebody helped her?"

"Sure did."

"Any ideas who?"

"Nope. He was ahead of her, climbing up, when she got there. I couldn't see him very well."

Mason thought about that for a moment.

"Should I...report this to...Burke?" Odin's inflection suggested that he did not like the idea.

"Not yet. We don't answer to him, and that ass wipe wouldn't do anything about it anyway. He's always schmoozing somebody in town, meetings and golf and shit." He waved his hand dismissively. "He's not much help to us."

"Right."

"But still...If the woman shows up again, I'll tell Burke about it then. She's got it in her head to be snooping where she shouldn't. And she has help. We need to get ready for that." Mason adjusted the shoulder holster for his revolver, a classic Colt Python.

"I'll be looking for them and when I find them, I'll need to hold them." Odin looked at Mason under his brow. "You know, to question them..."

"Among other things." Mason's eyes narrowed.

"We'll need someplace safe to keep them when I catch them." Odin pushed a fist into the palm of his hand.

"Right." Mason brightened. "Top story on the back of the old part of the inn."

"Good idea. Quiet. Away from everyone else."

"Second story. Make sure the window's nailed shut and get the door ready for a lock and chain."

"Already on it, boss."

CHAPTER 21

Relic checked the water in the pot as it boiled and dipped his knife into the rhizomes.

"We best get some food in you." He rummaged through a burlap bag and pulled out two plastic plates. "It's a little dusty, but clean." He handed one to her.

Wiping it with her shirt tail, she thought – it's a lot dusty and only a little clean, but it'll do.

He waved at her to lean toward the pot and dropped some of the cattail roots onto her plate. Steam billowed from the pieces, and when one was cool enough, she popped it into her mouth.

"Tastes a little like cucumber, but sweet," she said.

Relic nodded.

"I have to ask," she swallowed, "why did you help me?"

His eyes pinched, puzzled a bit by the question. "You obviously needed a hand."

"Well…"

"Now," he leaned forward, "let me tell you what I know." Relic recounted the men he'd saved from the flash flood in Demon's Roost, his discovery of the water pump at Sakwa Spring, the water tank, and his talk with Manny, the construction supervisor. "I think that big guy you were running from is the same one who confronted me below the spring. But then I got inside the original part of the inn and found something odd in a closet in there."

"What?"

"Hazmat suits. A row of them. With rubber boots on the floor below 'em."

"Why hazmat suits?" She stuffed another rhizome into her mouth. Not half bad, actually.

He shrugged and spread his hands, opening an imaginary atlas.

"Is there something about the construction? Something that would have them working with hazardous materials?" she asked.

"Maybe. Asbestos in the old inn?"

They finished the rest of the cattail, chewing and pondering the possibilities.

"Like it OK?" He pointed to the empty pot.

"Sick."

"It's making you sick?" He leaned forward, concern in his voice.

"No, no, 'sick,' like really good. Never had cat-tail before."

"Sick is good?"

"Sick is definitely good. Sick is cool."

"Healthy is still good, though, right?" He squinted at her.

She couldn't tell whether he was teasing or not, so she rolled her eyes and nodded. How long has this guy been in the outback? Since the nineties?

"So, you work at a newspaper? You're a reporter?" Relic leaned back.

"Sort of. Well, yes."

"Oh?"

"I'm finishing my degree in journalism but...had a hard time finding a real job, something I could sink my teeth into. I applied for an externship, where they subsidize a local newspaper to hire you, and got assigned here, to the Sentinel."

"A real job?"

"I wanted to stay near Seattle, do something really important..."

"But that's why you were watching the inn?"

"Yesterday was accidental. But then my editor sent me back to interview the boss there, the man named

Burke, to write a story about the project, the renovation."

Relic pulled a squished-up dinner roll from a pocket on the side of his cargo pants and held it in one hand. He pushed the plastic bottle he'd pulled from his cache and squeezed something into the bun.

"Want some?" He held it toward her.

"What is it?" Never mind, she scolded herself, just eat the damn thing. After the day she'd had, she could eat a horse.

"Bread with strawberry jam in the middle."

"Hell, yes." She took the bun and dug her teeth into it.

Relic made another one for himself.

She took her time with the soft, sweet desert and washed it down with water. That bread was pretty ugly, she thought. And a little gross. And wonderful.

Relic used the water left over from boiling the cattail to rinse the dishes and put it all away. He's more than just a guy out on a hike, she thought. With a camp like this, he's got to be staying here for stretches of time. What is he really doing way out here in the desert?

For that matter, what the hell was she doing way out here? Since she'd moved to that backwater town, she'd been sunburned, chased, exhausted, pulled up a cliff on a rope, witnessed a murder, and interviewed a killer. Well, a possible killer. She couldn't make up her mind about that guy.

Her thoughts swung quickly to her mother, her soft brown eyes, her laughter, her hugs. What would she do?

"You've lost someone close to you." Relic spoke the observation softly.

"How would you know?" Anger rose through her voice and she looked up at him, challenging him. Who the hell was he to say that?

Relic touched his eye and ran his finger down his cheek.

Shit. She'd been crying. She wiped her tears with the back of her hand and looked away from him.

"No shame in it." He fiddled with the wood in the fire. "We've all lost someone, you know."

"Covid…" she choked on the word.

"Me, too." He stirred a fresh stick into the flame. "A close friend…"

"I'm sorry. And you're right. I didn't mean to snap at you."

"Who did you lose?"

"My mother…" She took a breath. "She'd quarantined, worn her mask, kept her distance, but some guy without a face cover walked up behind her at the gas station, coughing and sneezing. Murder by Covid. They had no proof that he was the one who'd infected her, or even who he was, but it was the only thing that made any sense. Or no sense. People who thought they had a constitutional right to infect others – what the hell was up with that? I wanted to track that shithead down and flay him alive." She'd done little but cry for weeks.

Relic listened quietly.

"This move to a small-town newspaper was forced, my only option, really, and now it feels like my mom is even farther away from me than ever. I don't know if the distance will be good for me or bad for me. I wish I knew what my mother would do... I really don't know what I should be doing next."

"Look, I know you don't know me and it's hard to share thoughts at a time like this but..." he spread the palms of his hands.

"Yeah," she whispered, "go ahead."

"Your mother is still with you, a memory, sure, but much more than that. She persists, just – naturally. Lean on what she taught you and then do what *you* would do. I bet that's what she would want, so it's good that way, too. And when you get to the point where a memory of her makes you smile, you know you're going in the right direction."

She peered into the night beyond their little camp.

"Your mother – she lived a full life, I'd bet. A good one?"

"Of course." Her voice cracked. "But it was cut short…"

"Gandhi once said that a long life may not be good enough, but a good life is always long enough."

She pulled a ragged breath and released it slowly, an emotional sigh, and they sat quietly for some time. Stars appeared in a swath of sky visible beyond their sandstone cave, lights persisting in the darkness.

"May your memories be a blessing." Relic leaned forward, offering her a flask.

"Thanks." She took it and unscrewed the lid. It smelled vaguely like gin.

"Home made." He tossed more wood on the fire.

Why not? She let the drink slide down her throat, but it took some oxygen with it and she coughed. A long swallow of cool water calmed her tongue, so she took another shot of the muscled moonshine.

"Sick." She handed it back to Relic, who took a quick pull.

"So, what's your next move?"

The gin began to warm her stomach. "I'm not sure. I'm supposed to write a story about renovation of the inn…"

"Don't you want to report the murder to the sheriff?"

"I was going to report it to my boss, but he and the manager out there are golfing buddies."

"Now that's sick."

She grinned.

"But you have to report it."

"After all that's happened, well, what if I made a mistake? What if I saw something that looked like a murder but wasn't? I'd create a terrible mess. They'd have to tear up the foundation, maybe for nothing, and I'd probably lose my job before the first week."

"I thought this wasn't a real job anyway."

She shrugged. "It's all I have."

"You seem pretty sure about what you saw." Relic's dark eyes narrowed, light swirling across his face, shadows pulsing with the beat of the fire.

She stared into the flickering glow, thoughts drifting to her mother again. Sadness surged through her and she felt another tear drop onto her knee. Damn it.

The flames rose quickly along a freshly placed branch of wood.

"You'll always miss her, but it seems like there's something else there, too," Relic said.

Their little cave seemed to engulf them, a sandstone capsule surrounded by the void of space.

"Why her, you know? Why not me?"

"That's it." He sat straighter.

"What?"

"You're still angry at whoever gave her Covid, angry at those who spread the disease."

"Hell, yes, I'm angry."

Relic sat quietly for a moment. "We all get angry and rightfully so. It's OK for a while, but we have to channel that into doing something that is just and fair. The anger itself, well…"

"What?" She heard the edge in her voice.

"Holding onto anger is like drinking poison and expecting the other person to die. Buddha said that. Anger can tie you up in knots. It can take over your thoughts and poison them all. This is obvious. I'm not saying anything new, here…"

She felt his words float in the air.

"And you might be feeling a little guilty, too. You survived and your mother didn't."

"Guilty?"

"When we over-indulge guilt, we punish ourselves. For something we didn't do and can't change. If our compassion doesn't include ourselves, it's incomplete."

"I can't change how I feel about things," she

lashed at him.

They stared into the waving flames.

"What you think, you become. What you feel, you attract. What you imagine, you create."

Who the hell is this caveman?

"Give yourself a break. Let yourself heal up. And focus on what's ahead of you."

"It feels like I've been going through hell."

"Then you'd best not linger."

CHAPTER 22

Hailey had fallen asleep near the fire, legs tucked to her stomach, a fleece blanket over her chest. The scrape of metal on rock roused her from the deep. Sunrise swept in front of their little camp, a wave of light waking the rocks and grass and cliffs towering across the way.

"You made coffee?" She sat up and scratched her head.

Relic handed her a mug and she wrapped her fingers around its warmth.

"How?"

"Boil the coffee beans in water."

She took a careful sip.

"Be careful. Might put hair on your chest."

"No doubt."

"Bagels in the bag." He pointed.

She sunk her teeth into the stale bread, washing each bite with a sip of thick drink. She felt tired but refreshed. The coffee could make an elephant dance.

"You going to see the sheriff today?" He slid a heavy rock over his stash, the lid on prehistoric tupperware, all sandstone and dried mud.

"You think I should?"

"Up to you, of course. But you saw what you saw. It's better for you to face it than turn away." Relic stood and brushed himself off. "I'll be back." He walked away from the camp and out of sight.

She stared into her open hands, thinking. She didn't ask to see a man murdered and covered in concrete. She didn't want an externship at a yokel newspaper in the middle of nowhere. She didn't ask for a thug to chase her up a sandstone cliff. She hadn't asked for any of it and it angered her again.

She looked out across the narrow canyon to the cliffs opposite their little camp. Cracks and crags and ledges, random scars on the face of the bare rock, gave it a personality. Delicate blades of green rose from the ground, wiggling in the breeze, pliant against the implacable stone, the contrast a unique piece of art. The muscles in her neck relaxed a bit as she soaked in the feel of the place. A fraction of the universe, but with all the essential elements, right here in front of her.

She realized that she wasn't just focused on getting back to the city and the coast. She was focused on getting back in time, to when her mother was alive and her college classes were predictable and busy and the pandemic was just a prophecy. She had her memories of that, but of course she couldn't go back. No one could. The more she focused behind her, the more insurmountable the problems in front of her became, especially the ones she had to face now. She couldn't afford to divide her attention anymore. She was not going to get through this without setting some other things aside.

As a start, she was going to have to tell the sheriff what she'd seen.

Relic shuffled back into camp and sat across from her.

"How do I get to town from here?"

He tightened the hair in his ponytail. "We're north of the inn now. I can get you to a spot where you can walk the rest of the way down this canyon. The road to the old inn goes right past, so you can hitch a ride into town from there."

"You're not coming with me?"

"I'm going back...here..." He smoothed some dirt by the fire and drew in it with his finger. "Here we are, in Crooked Canyon. The next one downriver, south of here, is Bitterbrush Canyon – the one we climbed out of with the rope. Then, there's another canyon, Demon's Roost they call it, just south of the inn. That's where

I'm headed."

"Why go there?"

"I saw trucks driving past the construction site, not even slowing down, straight on down the road. Demon's Roost is a dry, narrow canyon. No Pueblo ruins, no petroglyphs, no water, just dry, dark rock that heats like a furnace in the summer. There's nothing to bring a bunch of people there, so I want to see what the attraction is."

"There's nothing past that gorge, where the trucks might go?"

"Nope. The river fills the main canyon below there. No place to put a road from there on, downriver."

"OK."

"And Hailey?"

"Yeah?"

"If you talk to the sheriff, would you avoid too many details about me and my little camp, here? I like my privacy."

He wore no hint of guile or deceit on his face and she thought, what the hell? She owed this caveman of the desert some thanks and some respect.

"Just…keep it to a minimum, if you can."

"Of course. You're like a confidential source on a news story."

"Perfect."

She finished her coffee, reached for her purse, and searched for her brush, placing lip gloss, lotion, and nail polish onto the ground. She found what she was looking for and blew loose sand out of the bristles. No need to look entirely like a cavewoman.

Relic organized his pack and handed her one of the water bottles.

"Won't you need this?"

"I have one. You can get that back to me another time."

She nodded, wondering when there would be another time. She put the bottle into her purse.

"Think those shoes'll get you back to town?" He pointed.

"Oh." Stitches along the insides of both shoes were pulled away from the soles, zig-zag threads over crescent-shaped smiles. They were hardly hiking boots. At least they weren't high heels. "Hope so."

"Follow me down." He walked away from the rock overhang and stopped.

She brushed her hair quickly and slung her purse strap over her shoulder. She stood slowly, her muscles protesting, and joined him outside the little camp. A wall of sunlit sandstone filled her view, fire on the ancient rock. The canyon was only a quarter of a mile wide at this spot, the ground peppered with red blossomed cacti, sage brush, and thin tufts of grass, patches of hair on an old man's head. It had a stark beauty to it, nothing like she'd ever seen before. She looked back at where they'd slept, a cozy bivouac tucked beneath a ledge. Barely noticeable even this close to it.

Relic led the way over sandy ground and rock. They soon reached a small spring, amazing to see in the middle of a rugged desert. Stalks of cattail grew along one side, the source of last night's dinner. Tall grass rimmed the edges, green spikes poking at the sky, something you'd expect in a swamp, but here they were clinging to the rarified moisture. A bowl of water rested in the center, maybe ten feet across, a lime-green film floating on the surface. A muddy path led to the pool on one side.

"Maybe coyote prints..." Relic pointed as they walked past.

"Crap." Two clear marks in the dirt, looking a lot like dog prints. "Is the coyote still around? Is it dangerous?" She hadn't thought about wild animals in this country. Had the coyote been watching them all along, lying in wait outside their little camp?

"He doesn't care about the two of us."

"We're OK, then?"

"Yep."

They walked another half-mile down the gorge. She scanned the cliffs and rocks above them, watching for the coyote that could be watching them.

The canyon widened dramatically and they approached a smooth, bare ridge, a polished rock where water must flow in a rainstorm. Relic removed his pack, pulled out his rope, and began to unwind it.

"Here," he handed one end to her. "Wrap this around, under your armpits."

"Another cliff?" She tied a double knot.

"A short one. The rope's just for safety. There's about twenty feet where it's slick as grease. Wouldn't kill you just from the fall, but you could get pretty hurt. Go ahead and climb down, but I've got you if you need a hand."

She peered over the edge and swallowed.

"Go ahead," he pointed.

She adjusted her purse over her head and shoulder and lowered herself to the ground, crawling to the edge.

"Go down facing the cliff. Feel your way with your feet as you go."

These kinds of risks were not in the tour book. She scrambled and scratched down the ledge, Relic holding firm on the rope. Her shoes slipped, her feet suddenly pedaling in thin air, a stab of panic through her chest, and she instinctively grabbed the rope. Relic lowered her a few more feet and she felt rocks beneath her toes again. A little more, and she was able to move the rest of the way down to the next level, a flattened area about fifty feet across. When she was solid on both legs, she pushed away from the cliff and untied herself.

"How are you going to get down?"

He leaned over the edge and pulled up his rope. "This is where we part ways, my friend."

"What?"

"Keep going down the canyon. It's not hard walking and it's not far – maybe two miles. It empties at the gravel road to the old inn."

"You sure you can't come with me?"

"Hitch a ride north, to your right as you leave this canyon. There are workers coming and going. Someone will take you into town."

"Shit." They'd talked about this, but still… Walking down the canyon all by herself. With shoes that were falling apart. And coyotes hiding in the shadows.

"Don't forget to see the sheriff."

"Where did you say you were going, again?"

"Straight to hell."

CHAPTER 23

Hailey stood outside the entrance to the county sheriff's office and hesitated. She'd hiked out of the canyon and found the dirt road where Relic had said it would be. As Relic had predicted, a pickup truck came by soon afterward and the driver gave her a lift into town.

She smoothed her hair, pulled her purse higher on her shoulder, and opened the door. She must look like a dust devil. With lipstick.

A wide countertop greeted the public, desks and phones and computers haphazardly arranged behind it. She found a silver "help" bell and rang it. A husky man in a tight uniform appeared from around the corner and approached, his leather belt squeaking with each step. The strap carried his pistol and small compartments shaped like compact envelopes. She wondered what was in them.

"Can I help you?" He examined her like an aristocrat eyeing a hobo, sizing her up in a glance, doubting her already.

She straightened her back and tightened her lips before she spoke. "I'm here to report a crime."

The officer gave a slow nod, still skeptical. "Do you need medical attention?"

"No."

"There's no one here that can help you at the moment, but you could come back in about an hour."

"An hour? It's urgent. I've seen…"

"…wait, there is someone who might help." His lips rose at the edges, lifted by something he found mildly humorous. He pointed to a door marked "Visitors" to her right. "Head in there and we'll get someone to you pronto."

"Sure." She went to the door and opened it.

"Dawson!" the officer yelled. "Intake up front for you!"

"Yeah?" a voice asked from around the corner.

"Another bigfoot sighting for you."

"Ha, ha."

She moved inside and sat across from a small table. The room had a wall clock and a stack of worn magazines by a sofa in the back. There were no windows, so she stared at a faded painting of ducks floating on a lake, mass-produced consumer art you'd find in a cheap hotel.

Another deputy strode into the room and extended his hand.

"I'm Dawson."

They shook hands. "I'm Hailey."

"What's going on today?" He sat across from her and smiled, a sort of outdoor, rocking chair friendly, hazel eyes clear and intent.

"What did the other deputy say about a bigfoot?"

Dawson shook his head. "It's an inside joke here. I've been looking for a moonshiner in Canyonlands for years, but the others say it's just a myth, a bigfoot. Never mind that."

"Oh."

"What can I help you with?"

She explained her externship at the Red Rock Sentinel then moved quickly to the man buried in concrete. Dawson leaned forward and questioned her for more detail, and she told him all she could. Then she told him about Martineau, her editor, going to a golf game with Burke, and her interview with Burke at the construction site.

She took a breath. Dawson started to ask something, but she raised a finger.

"Do you mind?" she pleaded. "Can I get through all of this first?"

"Sure." He sat back in his chair.

She told him how she'd gone into the basement of the old inn and the giant of a man who'd chased her deep into part of the foundation, the part built with stones, and how she'd escaped and ran into Bitterbrush Canyon. She said a man with a ponytail tossed her a rope and helped her get away for good.

Dawson sat up straight again.

Then she explained that he'd led her to a rock over-hang in Crooked Canyon, where they'd hid until today, when she'd walked out and hitched a ride into town.

She stopped for a moment and realized how thirsty she was. She reached into her purse, pulled out Relic's water bottle, and took a long swallow.

Then Dawson questioned her about all of it, but she explained that she'd been traumatized and exhausted and was a little fuzzy about the mystery man and just where in Crooked Canyon they'd found shelter. Though he seemed a little frustrated, he finally seemed satisfied and took a deep breath.

"So, what happens next?" She patted her hands against her knees.

"We investigate. You go home and…" he glanced at her "…get cleaned up and get some rest."

"What? That's it?"

"We'll stay in touch."

"You're going to go out there, right? I need to show you where the man was buried."

"You need to stay put for now."

Her stomach grumbled. The clock on the wall showed three thirty in the afternoon.

"And it would really help if you'd write up a statement for us. You're a reporter, right? Try to get it to us tomorrow morning."

She nodded, thinking about that. "Sure. Of course." But she couldn't help wondering if that was all she should do. What would her mother say? Should she stay in town? Or find a way to get back to the old inn, do what a reporter should do?

But how? Her Blazer was parked at the trailer houses below the construction site.

Dawson rose from his seat and waved his hand toward the door. "I've gotta go, so I'll let you see yourself out."

"OK."

Dawson hurried out of the room and the problem stumped her. She stared at the wall until she thought of Ash, the photographer, the guy she'd dumped coffee on yesterday morning. She couldn't do a real story without some pictures of the place.

****

Relic hiked back to his camp. He found a bottle of Hailey's nail polish on the ground as he passed and tucked it into his pack. He travelled on, taking most of the day to reach Demon's Roost, past the old inn and past the spring. He made his way through a tumble of rocks on the rim and settled into a spot where he could see most of the barren gorge. He set his pack on the ground and pulled out his binoculars.

He found the gravel road at the mouth of the canyon and followed it as it wound toward him. The road disappeared from view for a bit, hidden by part of the canyon rim, and became visible again closer to him, deeper into the gorge.

"Shit on a shingle."

A new white and orange backhoe sat unattended next to an open trench, its stabilizers spread like the legs of a flightless bird, the dipper resting its bucket on the ground, an ostrich head at rest. The excavation was maybe twelve feet wide and forty yards long, all new, all put there after the flash flood a few weeks ago. He adjusted his binoculars. Round, tubular objects lined part of the trench, looking a lot like fifty-gallon metal drums.

He had a thought about what those might be, what they might mean, and his breath caught in his throat.

CHAPTER 24

She ran from the sheriff's office, out the door, and across the street, making her way toward the newspaper offices. She hoped to hell Ash was around.

The door rang its little bell when she opened it. Inside, Ash was seated at a desk, staring at a computer screen.

"Hey, Ash." She waved as she approached the front counter.

He looked up, a bit startled to see her.

No one else was at the front – she could see two women in a back office talking with each other.

She waved at him to come over, quickly.

He looked about, stood from his chair, and made his way to the front.

"Hailey?"

"Ash, I need your help, right away."

"Are you OK?"

"Yeah, but a huge story is going to get away from us if we don't get a move on, right now."

He squinted at her, his question implicit.

"Come on, now, right now, I can tell you about it outside."

He glanced at the women in back, grabbed his camera, and moved to the end of the counter, where the swinging door let him move into the public space. He approached her, a look of concern pinching his brow.

She spun and waved at him to follow. She opened the door and slid to a stop.

Mr. Martineau stood outside, waiting for them to exit.

"Hailey? Where've you been? Where's your piece on the new inn?"

What? She had an instant to decide whether to explain herself or keep plowing forward. She reached behind her and grabbed Ash's hand.

"Hello, sir, sorry to rush but we've going to finish that story and you'll be so very pleased with it." She pushed past him, Ash in tow.

Ash shrugged his shoulders at Martineau as they passed.

They hurried down the street to the next corner and turned to get out of Martineau's sight. Ash stopped, jerking her to a halt.

"What the hell? You look like you've been in a rock tumbler or something."

"Ash, we've gotta get out to the inn. Listen, we need to take your car." She reached for his hand again and tugged him along. "Where is it?"

"Hailey, you have to tell me what the hell is going on."

"I've seen a murder out there and they buried the guy in cement. When I went into the basement of the old part of the inn, a man the size of a fullback chased me through a tunnel and into a box canyon and I barely got away. I've told Deputy Dawson my story and he's headed out there now."

Ash's eyes rounded into blue-white marbles.

"We need to show him where the man was murdered and we need to get some good shots, some pictures of the place." She walked backward, away from him, waving him to come along. He gave his head a quick nod, lips tight, and pointed across the street to an old Toyota pickup truck. They were soon in the cab, Ash dropping the keys from above the visor. They drove toward Main Street.

"Food." She pointed at the drive-through and Ash followed her direction. He ordered a large burger and she ordered two.

They drove quickly through town and down the highway toward the country road that led along the river.

She'd never tasted a greasy burger so wonderful. When she was done with the first, she tucked the other into her purse, released a small belch, and told Ash what had happened in more detail.

He pushed the gas pedal to the floor.

CHAPTER 25

Burke led Deputy Dawson to the old hotel office and pointed to the chair Hailey had sat in the day before. "Have a seat, officer, and tell me what this is all about."

Burke's mug had been on his desktop since seven this morning, but he took a sip of the cold coffee anyway. The only reasons for a visit from the sheriff's office were not good ones, and the deputy seemed especially tense. Burke was going to have to react quickly, and calmly, to whatever came next. He lowered himself into his swivel chair.

Dawson sat on the edge of the other chair, leaning forward. "We have a report of a death here at the construction site."

"What?" Burke stiffened his back.

"Happened a couple of days ago, where the foundation is going in for that new section you're working on."

"No, that can't be true. We all would know about

something like that, I mean..."

"There's more to it than that." Dawson was watching him closely.

Burke narrowed his eyes and put his hands on the arm rests.

"The man was murdered, in fact, and buried in concrete."

"What the hell!" He stood quickly, shoving the chair behind him.

Dawson stood, one hand near the holster on his belt.

"Shit," Burke turned away from the deputy, shaking his head. "What proof of this do you have?"

"Eyewitness."

Damn it to hell. Someone had seen the killing. Think, man, and think fast. What do I tell this deputy? How do I keep things from going to hell, from it all unravelling?

"How reliable is this witness?" He turned back toward Dawson, who held his ground.

"Reliable enough." His lips pressed tightly together, an accusation.

Well, shit. Burke stared at the deputy, knowing a decision had to be made. Right then.

He shook his head and slumped his shoulders for

a moment, then moved back into his chair. "Deputy…" he put his hands together on top of the desk in front of him. "I'm afraid I'm going to have to come clean with you. And ask for your discretion."

Dawson canted his head. "I'm listening."

Burke sighed. "I learned about the murder yesterday." He kneaded his fingers together. "I couldn't do anything to prevent it, see, I'm not in the chain of command for security around here. Well…I'd best start at the beginning."

Dawson sat on the edge of his chair, patient but taut.

"I'm going to read you into this, and when I'm done, you'll have to agree to keep all of it quiet."

The deputy crossed his arms against his chest, a silent refusal to agree to anything.

"My real name is Jeff Colby. I'm a special agent with the FBI, assigned undercover to investigate an L.A. crime family, a syndicate that operates out of L.A., Phoenix, and Salt Lake."

Dawson's brow rose.

"Yes, there is organized crime in Salt Lake City. And this particular endeavor brings them to an out-of-the-way enterprise along the Colorado River, off the beaten path. We don't know why, yet. But they're smart and ruthless. And organized like a terrorist group, complete with separate cells that don't always know what the others are really doing. My job is to be the front man, so to speak. The guy who gets the local permits, makes friends with the other businesses, makes legitimate management decisions for the hotel."

Dawson seemed more skeptical than ever.

"Wait. Let me get you some proof of who I am. I have sort of a letter of introduction, in case I need to call on local law enforcement for help."

"Yes?"

"It's taped to the outside bottom of the bottom drawer of my desk." He pointed downward. "Can I pull it out slowly and set it on the desk for you?"

Dawson nodded, unsnapping his holster and putting his right hand onto his pistol grip.

Burke held up his hands, then let his left reach to the empty drawer. He pulled it out of the desk and lifted it slowly upward, turning it so Dawson could see both sides. On the bottom, a pale envelope was taped to the wood. Burke set the drawer on the desktop, peeled the envelope away and handed it to the deputy.

Dawson nodded at him to raise his hands again.

Burke sat quietly, hands in the air, as Dawson removed a business card from the envelope. It carried a raised blue and gold seal, the scales of justice on a shield in the middle.

"The name and phone number are who you call to verify the undercover operation."

"I need more than this."

"I can't exactly keep my FBI photo I.D. on me, now can I? I've kept this card hidden for nearly nine months and now that I've used it, you need to keep it."

"Agent Colby?"

"At your service." He lowered his hands to the desk. "But you'd best keep calling me Mr. Burke."

CHAPTER 26

They heard a *tap-tap* on the door.

Burke looked to Dawson and mouthed the words "call that number." He tucked the empty envelope into his pants pocket, put the drawer back on its rollers, and slid it into place.

"Yes?"

Dawson put the business card into his shirt pocket.

A man opened the door and peeked inside. "Got a minute?"

"Sure." Burke stood and motioned for Dawson to do the same. "We're done here. Sheriff, meet Mason, our security chief."

"Deputy sheriff," he corrected, extending his hand. They shook.

"Problem?" Burke asked Mason.

"Contractor issue, yeah."

"Let's go out." Burke waved toward the door.

Mason left the room. Burke followed, then Dawson.

They walked through the hotel lobby and into the bright sunlight. Mason strolled a respectful distance away and waited for Burke and Dawson to say goodbye.

"Nice meeting you." Burke patted Dawson on the shoulder then shook hands with him. "Come by again, if you really need to." He put a subtle emphasis the word "really."

"Interesting project you have here." Dawson looked up at the building.

"Yes. Even if it is a little outside of your jurisdiction." Burke looked Dawson in the eye then turned and walked toward Mason. The two of them walked along the side of the new addition.

"What did he want?" Mason whispered.

"Somebody reported the theft of a circular saw, of all things. I told him we'd ask around, but tools have a way of disappearing sometimes."

"Well, we've got an issue."

Burke looked at him.

"That woman who we found searching the basement? The one Odin chased into the canyon but got away?"

"Yes…"

"She's back on site and has some guy with her,

snapping pictures."

Burke stopped. "Where?"

Mason looked past the cinder block walls, toward the house trailers used by the contractors, then scanned toward the mouth of Bitterbrush Canyon. "There," he pointed.

They were probably a half-mile away, off the end of the foundation, talking to each other, keeping their heads down. Burke recognized her immediately – the new reporter from the Red Rock Sentinel.

"Odin and I will take care of them. Just so you know." He nodded at Burke, a statement of fact, a directive that he not interfere.

CHAPTER 27

"We need some shots of the old part of the inn, over here." Hailey walked to their left. They'd moved through the stacks of lumber and past the workers to the corner of the new section, the foundation where she'd seen the man buried in concrete. They'd moved as inconspicuously as they could, but of course they'd been noticed.

Ash moved to their right and squatted, lining up a shot of the inn, the carpenters and masons at their tasks.

"Come on, Ash, hurry up. This is photojournalism, not art class."

"The best photojournalism *is* art." He changed the angle of his camera and clicked again.

"Let's go once around then get the hell out of here."

"Coming."

She figured if the guard caught them, they'd say they'd arrived with the deputy, who would be giving them a ride back to town. Still, she did not want another encounter with the man who'd chased her out of the cellar – he gave her the absolute creeps. If the deputy caught them, they'd have no excuse, but she didn't think he'd arrest her for interfering with his investigation. They were reporters after all, reporting on the fabulous renovation of the historic inn. He could even check with her editor.

They walked briskly to the south, downriver and past the new part of the building to the place she'd emerged from the old basement. She pointed and Ash snapped a few pictures. They worked their way up the slope, level with the height of the second story of the original part of the inn. Ash took more pictures of the clapboard siding, the sagging roof, the restored portions in stark contrast with the old.

"Up here." Hailey motioned them higher until they reached a level trail that led farther south. She heard the faint click of the camera behind her and turned around quickly.

"What are you doing?"

He shrugged. "My job."

"No pictures of the reporter needed."

"Well OK, then." He sounded a little peeved.

"Looks like a water tower there." She pointed.

Ash took some photos of the metal cistern and the wooden scaffolding that supported it.

A small engine puttered in the distance.

"Up here. Here's the spring I told you about." The one Relic had told her about. She hurried along the wide path as it turned uphill and climbed to a dirt road next to the pump. No one else seemed to be nearby.

Ash stopped to catch his breath and snapped a few pictures of the gasoline engine and the hoses, one leading toward the inn, one draped into the little spring, nearly all of its water sucked dry.

Hailey watched the engine rumble in place and remembered what Relic had said about the importance of the spring to the life of this canyon.

"Oh!" She jumped at a nudge against her knee and glanced down. A dog sat in the dust next to her, its ears pointed up but for their tips, which drooped a little, its brown eyes intent on hers.

"Hey, Ash." She knelt toward the dog, cautious at first. But it seemed like a grown-up puppy, poking its black nose toward her then backing away. The dog was making sure Hailey was safe to approach, so she slowly offered her hand for it to smell. She could hear Ash taking a couple of pictures of it.

The animal moved closer and she rubbed it between the ears, which seemed to release a flood of emotion, the dog stroking against her, prancing about. It looked like a cross between a border collie and something else, its fur the shade and pattern of a coyote's. She thought of the animal tracks she and Relic had seen in the other canyon.

"It smells your hamburger." Ash pointed to the dog.

"Oh, it's hungry for sure." She reached into her purse and pulled out the fast food, but instead of grabbing at it, the dog sat again, staring at the bun.

"It's a polite thing, isn't it?" Ash said.

She unwrapped the burger and reached forward with it. The dog placed his mouth around it gently, then took the food and swallowed it in three quick bites, licking its lips.

"Hungry thing." Hailey stood up again.

Suddenly, the dog turned away from them and snarled.

The giant of a man who'd chased her through the basement and into the canyon stood twenty feet away, arms crossed, staring at them. Lying to him about arriving with the deputy suddenly seemed hopelessly stupid.

"Hey, Ash." She tugged on his shirt sleeve and he looked up.

"Thanks, but we'll find our own way home," Ash spoke quickly to the man.

They turned to scurry down the trail but stopped cold.

Another man blocked their way, pistol in hand.

CHAPTER 28

Dawson went straight to his desk back at the office and fired up his computer. He went to the FBI database and typed the name of the man on the business card Burke had given him. There it was – supervising agent out of Salt Lake City. The phone number on the card matched the one on the FBI directory. Damn. He'd been hoping it was fake. Burke was a bit of an ass, but then, maybe that fit the mold.

If he was being really suspicious, or vindictive, or just angry at federal interference, he'd call the man's supervisor. Nobody should cover up a murder in his county, not even an undercover agent. Even if he was just being thorough, he told himself, he ought to make the call.

After punching numbers for a computer-generated system, he eventually reached a live person, who took his information and put him on hold.

"Mitchell here." The man's voice was clipped,

impatient.

Dawson again explained who he was and that he'd spoken with an agent Colby, who'd given him Mitchell's contact information.

"What did the agent tell you?"

"Not much. That there's a federal investigation, he's been undercover for nine months or so, it's at a delicate stage, and I should please stay away from the old inn. What is he investigating? Is this legitimate?"

"I can't tell you what's under investigation, but, yes, we have that agent in the field."

"Does whatever's going on present a threat to the county? To our residents?"

"You must know how this works, sheriff..."

"...deputy..."

"Right. Agent Colby must have felt it was necessary to brief you on the investigation, so you'd know to stay clear of it, but that's all I'm authorized to tell you. Anything else today, sheriff?"

"No."

"Thanks for checking in." The phone went dead.

"Thanks for nothing." Dawson slapped the receiver back onto its cradle.

CHAPTER 29

Relic scooted away from the edge of the high cliff until the barrels at the bottom of Demon's Roost were out of view. He stood and packed his binoculars away. Restless, he wound his way through loose rocks and back along the route he'd taken from the main canyon, back toward Broken Inn.

An early summer sun baked the earth, silence filling the air, all the animals but man deep in their burrows or shaded nests. He moved at an easy lope for more than an hour, until he reached the rim above Sakwa Spring. From there, he walked an old game trail to a short ledge. He lowered himself down the slope and resumed his trek, watching for any sign of people near at hand. Thunderstorms slid across the sky, moving toward him from the west. Wisps of rain fell from the clouds, curling upward before they reached the earth, evaporating before they could cool the heated sands.

The ground levelled out here, still high enough to block most of his view of the inn. After a while, the flats dropped off again to a small switchback leading the rest of the way to the spring, but he saw people there, next to the water pump. He could hear the engine – they'd replaced it again. He lay on the edge, only his head above the rim.

He was close enough to see without his binoculars. The large security man stood still as a statue, watching Hailey and a young man with her, who was petting a dog. Another security guard walked up slowly behind them. Hailey and her friend were startled by the giant of a man, turned quickly, and stopped in front of the other man.

The large man moved closely behind Hailey, leading her down the path toward the old part of the inn. The other guard moved behind Hailey's friend and the two of them shuffled as if they were on their way to the gallows.

When they all reached the south side of the old inn, the original part, they entered through a door on the end. When it closed behind them, Relic slid down the steep path to the pump and stopped for a breath.

Once again, the spring was nearly dry.

He decided to try something different. The tubes on each end were clamped tightly to the pump, but with some twisting, he was able to loosen them, water now leaking around the edges. He removed the one on the uphill side, so that the pump was sucking only air, the system surging and bucking, an intestinal disaster. Then he slid off the tube on the downhill side, relieving its distress, and turned the pump around. He re-attached first the tube to the spring, then the second tube to the water tower, tightening them with his fingers. He hoped there was enough water in the tubes to prime the pump.

The engine continued to rumble, but now, in reverse position, it pumped water from the tower back into the spring. He watched for a moment to make sure the maneuver had worked. Unless they looked closely, they'd see and hear the pump working like it should. Only when their water tower was empty, only when their water for concrete ran dry, would they suspect they had a problem. By then, the little spring would be full and it would take hours or days to pump it out again.

He took a long drink of water and considered the fact that Hailey and her companion had not reappeared.

CHAPTER 30

Hailey flinched when the giant shoved Ash hard against the wooden floor. Ash crawled away until his back stopped against the frame of an old bed, but the man stepped forward and back-handed him across the cheek, twisting his face away from her. Ash groaned, and the muscles in her back seemed to melt. The giant tied Ash's hands behind his back then lashed them to the wooden frame. The man pulled the camera from around Ash's neck and, though he tried to resist, the effort was futile.

The other man took a step closer to her, six-shooter at her forehead, bullets visible in their chambers. Until then, she'd only seen guns in the movies. Frost seemed to build behind her eyes as she stared at the naked barrel and the bleak projectiles. The man waved his pistol toward the floor and she sat across from Ash, next to the other bed post. The giant took her purse then tied her hands behind her and to the post, as he'd done with the photographer.

They sat on the floor of the old inn, each tied to separate ends of the same wooden frame. The mattress had probably been discarded years ago. There was one window, but it was boarded up, a sloppy job that let daylight filter inside the stale room.

The two men glanced at them and then each other. The man with the gun gave a quick nod and they left the dilapidated room. Hailey could hear the rattle of a chain against the door, no doubt locking them inside.

"Damn it." She shoved her back against the frame, sliding it a few inches into the wall, jarring her head. "Ow."

"Easy…"

"I'll 'easy' those guys right in the ass."

"How am I tied? Can you see the rope and the knots?" Ash leaned forward.

She took a breath, trying to clear her anger and looked at him. His hands were tied together tightly, and the rope looped around the bed post above and below where it joined the frame. It would not be possible to slip it over or under the post. He jammed it downward, then upward, but the knots held firm.

"It's no use." She heard the dejection in her own voice.

They sat for a while, staring at the pine-board floor in front of them. The hotel room was bare of carpet and any furniture other than the bed frame. Dust motes swam in a shaft of light from the window. Mice feces spread randomly along the wall to the bathroom, its door removed, the inside oozing an odor she did not want to identify.

Above, the inside ceiling had long ago been pulled down, exposing rafters and the underside of the roof. Sunlight shined through a hole the size of a couple of basketballs.

"God, I'm hungry." Ash spoke into the emptiness.

"How can you be hungry at a time like this?"

"We had an extra hamburger." His lips rose at the edges, an effort at some humor.

"Yeah, well, the dog made short work of that."

"Hope its stomach's full and it's resting well. It owes us one."

"It should've been a rescue dog," she huffed.

"I don't think that's what 'rescue dog' means."

"I know."

"You're right, though. We should've trained it to unlock doors and chew through ropes." He yanked on his restraints.

"Yeah…"

"They took my camera." He looked to his chest, where the camera had been.

"Yeah, but that's the least of our worries. These guys just kidnapped us. At gun point!"

"You said they'd killed a man and put him in concrete."

"Yeah. I figured we were safe with the police out here."

"Me, too. Plus with all the carpenters and workers around," Ash said.

"I guess we got too far away from them all."

"Martineau knows we came out here, so they can't keep us here forever. What are they going to do? Hide us from our own newspaper editor?"

They sat quietly for a moment.

"Wait…" They'd followed the deputy to the site, but he'd left the building with Burke, patting his shoulder, shaking his hand, just walking away. It hadn't really made an impression on her until now. She looked at Ash from under her brow.

"What?"

"What if they tell the sheriff some tall tale about us and he believes them? Martineau would go along with the sheriff, wouldn't he?" she asked.

Ash nodded slowly.

"Burke was pretty friendly with Deputy Dawson."

"Yeah, but…"

"And if they sink us in concrete, who's to say we didn't wander off into the desert or something?" Hailey stared at the locked door.

"Well, you're a fountain of optimism, aren't you?"

CHAPTER 31

Relic stayed high above the inn, moving toward the mouth of Bitterbrush Canyon and the north side, the new part of the project. He found one of the security team, the shorter man, making his way toward the three house trailers, stopping to look around from time to time. The giant was nowhere he could see. Relic squatted behind a rock and watched some more.

A semi-truck loaded with wooden tresses had backed in toward the new foundation. He assumed the triangular frames would go atop the walls of the new addition as support for a roof. Four men unloaded them, one at a time, and stacked them on the ground a few yards away.

Thunder rumbled in the distance, quaking the air. Dark clouds suddenly dimmed the sun, erasing shadows, making the early evening feel later than it was. Rain would sweep through pretty soon, he thought.

Once unloaded, the truck pulled away and back down the road toward the trailer houses. Men began to put tools into their belts, following the semi away from the site. Supper time. He still hadn't seen Hailey or her friend since they'd gone into the abandoned part of the inn.

He had a random thought.

No one was near the tresses, so he slid down the slope and walked boldly toward them, just another worker on his way to dinner. When he reached the stack, he ducked behind them. He slipped out his hunting knife and began shaving strips off the two-by-fours into a little pile at his feet. Soon, he had a handful of pine slivers and flakes positioned beneath one of the boards. He lit a match under the detritus and blew gently until the flame took hold.

Clangs and dismembered voices swam through the air as people continued to make their way toward the mess hall. The feel of oncoming rain seemed to hurry everyone along.

Soon, the nearest tress was solidly aflame, reaching toward others in the stack. He walked quickly toward the cinder block walls of the new addition and ran along the back of the inn toward the old part of the building. He counted the boarded-up windows as he passed, ten of them in all. He stopped at the corner and looked back.

Fire had swept into the tresses, smoke rising into the air. Soon enough, someone would see it.

He rounded the corner and there, all alone, sat the dog he'd seen earlier with Ash and Hailey.

"Hey there."

The dog wagged its tail so hard its hips moved with it.

Relic rubbed its head. "Gotta check in here," he whispered. He held his hand toward the dog in a command for it to wait.

Relic opened the door slowly and peeked inside. Down the old hotel were a series of doorways, mirror image sentries along the hallway, retired long ago. A staircase rose to his left, leading to the second story. He thought he heard creaks and thumps above, so he treaded carefully up the steps. He peered around the corner at the top.

The hallway was empty. A heavy layer of dust coated electric sconces along the walls. Natural light leaked through a window at his end of the hall, one of the only ones not boarded up.

The first door on the right had a chain and lock across it, obviously new. The iron links wrapped firmly around and across the door, anchored to wooden studs nailed into sides of the frame. Without a crowbar, and the noise that went with it, there was nothing he could do to get it open. He heard voices inside, talk of dogs and hamburgers and sheriffs. He could say something to them, but he'd have to yell, which might bring one of the security guards.

He thought for a moment or two then slid his pack to the floor. He opened the window at the end of the hall and leaned out, checking above him for places to grasp. Satisfied, he moved back inside and searched his pack until he found the bottle of clear nail polish Hailey had forgotten at their camp. "Fast Dry," it said on the label. He set that beneath the lock and removed a pack of matches. He tore off the back, folded it into a "v" shape, and held it against the lock. Then he opened the polish and poured it down the make-shift funnel into the mechanism until it was full. He balanced the lock against the door, upside down so the goo would stay inside until it dried. He put the cap back on the polish and put it and the matches away. He tossed the "v" part of the cardboard against the opposite wall and crept back to the window at the end of the hallway.

The old nail-polish-in-the-lock trick was step one.

CHAPTER 32

The roof was about three feet from the top of the window, a reach he could make if he stood on the bottom of the frame. Relic tightened the straps on his pack and stepped out, toes on the edge of the wood, hands clutching the upper casing.

Thunder rumbled through the air.

He reached one hand to the roof and tugged along the edge, testing its strength. The shingles on the old part of the inn were some kind of wooden shake, originally thick and solid but now gray and cracked. Once on top, he'd have to trust them and the old framing underneath.

He worked his fingers under the shingles, holding onto the structure below. When he felt solid, he slid his other hand a little higher on the roof line and lifted himself in a chin-up. Then he swung his right leg up to the lower part of the roof and rolled onto the angled surface.

White smoke wafted over him, sounds of men

shouting in the distance. They'd found the burning tresses and were probably putting them out.

He peeked back over the brink. The dog he'd seen earlier was still seated at the bottom of the first-floor doorway, looking straight up at him, a question in its eyes.

"Quiet," he whispered.

Relic rolled away from the edge and crawled along the slope of the roof. There it was – the hole in the ceiling he'd seen earlier. He figured it was over the hotel room on this end of the building, the one with the chain and lock on the door.

****

Hailey stared at the closed door, the only exit from the room, and wondered about the deputy, her editor, and Burke, the man who seemed to have an influence over them. And the ropes chaffing against her wrists. If these men would kill someone and bury them in concrete once, they sure as hell could do it again. Their only problem was doing it without getting caught, a problem that arose only after she and Ash were long dead. She suddenly missed her mother again, the sadness creeping like a vine across her line of sight. Then she realized it was something else.

A vertical cord dropped before her, a knife tied to the end of it, the thing so foreign and weird her mind could not immediately process it. It slid gently down until the tip of the blade touched the wooden floor, spun sideways, and caught the light, some magic sword from the days of King Arthur. She found herself staring at it for some time, then following the rope upwards, all the way to the hole in the roof, where a man with a dark goatee peered down at them, into the cave of a dragon.

She straightened her back and whispered to Ash, urging him to stay quiet, but to look up at Relic, quickly. His eyes registered bald surprise.

"Cut yourselves loose," Relic spoke from above. The rope lifted the knife again and he slowly swung it back and forth, away and forward, until momentum slid it toward the back of her hands. Her fingers reached and reached, then wrapped around the handle, but she could not see where to cut.

"Higher," Ash insisted. "No, over toward the wall some more."

She could feel the tension of the rope beneath the blade.

"That's good. Just saw it back and forth. Be careful."

In moments, she'd cut the part of the rope that tied her to the bedpost. She scooted away, slid her bound hands underneath her legs, so they were in front of her, and grabbed the knife again. She moved to Ash and sliced through the knot that bound his hands. He quickly took the knife from her and cut away the rope that held her wrists.

"Send the knife back up," came Relic's voice from above.

Hailey set the knife on the floor then watched it rise through the rafters. In moments, the rope lowered again, this time with two loops of webbing material attached part way up the rope.

"We have to climb up?" Hailey whispered to Relic.

"Yes…" Ash interrupted, stepping to the rope, "… but we have Prusik loops." He pointed to the straps. "You put one foot in each and hold onto the climbing rope above you with your hands. Each loop will slide up the rope when you lift your foot. Think of it like a stair master. Lift one foot up, then when you put your weight on that foot and push down, it will grip. Then lift the other foot, and so on."

She stared at them for a moment.

"My friends and I do some rock climbing for fun," Ash said.

"Hey, whatever it takes."

"I'm heavier than you, so I'll anchor the rope and

you go up first," Ash handed her one of the waist-height loops. "Keep your right foot in this one, your left in that other one, and move them up on the rope, one at a time."

"I see." She grabbed the rope above her head and placed her right foot into the highest loop. When she lifted her left foot from the floor, she swung awkwardly on the rope until she could fit her left foot into the empty loop. Then she pulled that foot upward. When she had her left leg as high as she could get it, she shifted her weight onto that and stood up on it. Then she lifted her right foot, keeping it in the right loop. She slid her hands above as she went, using them to pull, too, and to stay upright. She rested her weight on both loops for a moment and repeated the process. Ash wrapped the rope around his arms and leaned back, straightening the braid for her, making the climb more controlled.

She swayed back and forth as she rose, slowly getting the hang of it, but her hands ached, her arm muscles straining with every reach and pull. Sweat rolled down her temples and armpits as the exertion took its toll. When she reached the rafters, she wrapped her left arm around the horizontal support and caught her breath.

"Almost home," Relic said from a few feet above.

She moved the right loop higher and pulled up again and again and finally she reached the top of the tress. Relic had tied the rope there but also had some of it wrapped around his waist as a brace. She reached her left hand through the hole in the roof and slid both arms onto the outer surface. Relic grabbed her behind the shoulders and tugged her higher onto the roof. She swung her legs over the top, rolled to a stop, and stared into the gray clouds in the sky, panting.

She could hear Ash straining up the rope, rafters creaking against the swing of his weight. Relic helped him onto the roof and he, too, lay back to catch his breath.

Relic leaned over the hole, untied the rope, then wound it all into a neat oval and tied it off, loops still attached. He stuffed it all into the bottom of his pack and put it back onto his shoulders.

Ash sat up. "Amazing, man."

"Ash meet Relic, Relic meet Ash," Hailey pointed at one and then the other.

Relic nodded at Ash and stepped toward the end of the roof, toward the spot he'd climbed from the window. A dog yipped beneath them. Relic leaned over the edge then snapped his head backward.

"Hey!" A man shouted from below.

CHAPTER 33

"Security," Relic whispered, pointing down toward the ground.

Hailey could hear a door open and slam shut on the first floor.

"They can't get into your room, so that might confuse them, delay them a little," Relic said, moving carefully over the old roof. "But they might come up the same way I did, so we'd best get going."

Hailey stood slowly, leaning into the angle of the roof so that she stood erect. She crawled past the hole a bit and rested in a squat position, hands on the shingles for extra stability. The sky was dark with rain, wind whipping through her hair, little to hold onto.

The shingle under Ash's boot suddenly broke away from the roof and he dropped quickly to his knees, one leg sprawled out behind him, hands atop the apex of the roof, the wooden shingle spinning down across the rest of them and out into the air, past the roof line, and out of view.

Another gust of wind plastered Hailey's shirt to her chest, bringing with it the faint smell of charred wood.

Relic moved past her and Ash and turned back toward them. "I'll go ahead. Let's get to the repaired section, where the roof is solid, and try to find a way down from there. Stand on opposite sides and hold hands as you go across."

Ash crawled over the top and onto the other side of the slope and looked at Hailey. She stood carefully and went to him. Ash held his hand to her elbow and she held hers to his, each balancing on opposite sides of the ridge. They walked in unison, following Relic.

The old part of the inn was longer than she'd thought from seeing it at a distance. They had maybe forty yards to go to reach the new section, where the rafters and plywood had been stabilized or replaced. The wind picked up again, hurtling tiny drops of rain against her face, stinging her cheeks. She tried to keep her eyes on her feet and stay even with Ash.

Thunder split the air above.

A torrent of cold rain smacked hard against their heads, soaking her shoulders, tingling her scalp. Her feet slid quickly beneath her, slick on the dampened shingles, and her whole weight dropped downward. She squeezed tightly against Ash's arm and felt him slide down with her, her elbow cracking against the roof line, her legs stretched helplessly beneath her, ready to pull her all the way down the slope. She reached for Ash's arm with her other hand and held tight.

"Try to stand up again," Ash's voice wavered under the pounding rain. She nodded and braced herself on his arm, cycling her legs against the shingles until she found some purchase. She stood unsteadily, sliding her feet under her weight, afraid they would skid out again with any miscalculation. Ash stood, too, and they began to walk again across the wet rooftop.

The rain continued to pour. Relic was ahead of them, walking with one foot on each side of the ridge and though he could not have been far away, the storm nearly hid him from view.

She shuffled each step as they went, remembering the slick soles on her shoes, the tops pulling away from the bottoms, and hoped they would not fall apart on her.

Another crack of thunder split the air and the shingles under her right foot slid quickly down the slope, pulling her hard to her knees. She turned toward Ash again, holding tighter than ever and he stopped her slide. She tried to shake the water from her eyes and pulled her legs under her weight again, preparing to stand. She nodded at Ash and checked behind them.

The giant was crawling steadily across the ridge, straight for them.

CHAPTER 34

"Oh, god." Her voice disappeared into the beating rain. She stood and shuffled across the shingles, feet skating forward quickly, leading Ash along with her. She forced herself not to look backward until they neared the fresh plywood, the repaired part of the roof, when a grunt behind her made stop and twist to see. Ash kept moving, tugging her arm, but when she saw the big man behind her, fear locked her joints into place, dread freezing her right there, dismay pulsing like a beating heart.

The man's hair clung to his forehead, dark fingers wrapping against his face, water dripping from his nose and chin, shirt fused with his muscled chest. His eyes narrowed and he swung his arms forward, a reach just shy of her neck. She wanted to scream but she couldn't, her mind spellbound, her voice stalled with shock.

Ash pulled at her arm.

The giant flung his hands toward her again, leaning into the reach this time, his eyes determined, teeth clenched. Just then, as he bent closely into her, his right foot slipped and he kneed onto the ridgeline with a crack, arms twirling, and the shingles beneath his left leg slid downward, a single unit of slick, rotten wood. His eyes bulged in surprise and he reached for purchase on the ridge, but the rain made it all slick as oil, his muscles, his weight, tugging him suddenly and certainly downward. He pounded his hands into the shingles but now the wood was sledding with him like a sheet of ice on ice, an avalanche he had no way to brake, the rasp of acceleration inevitable, and he launched right off the edge, suddenly weightless and then out of sight.

He hit the ground with the sickening slap of a wet towel.

"Come on." Ash tugged her arm again.

The rain fell in a torrent now and she stood there, staring at the bare wood beneath the shingles that had taken the man to the ground below them. She turned to look at Ash, his face barely visible even so close to hers, the rain in her eyes and ears, every part of her as drenched as if she were swimming in whitewater rapids. She took a tentative step forward, then another, letting Ash lead them to the newer part of the roof, where the wood was still slick, but solid.

The sky broke for a moment, the downpour passed, and they came to the end of the roof. She no longer smelled burnt wood. This rain would have doused most fires and driven firefighters to shelter. Still, there were men about and they'd have to keep a lookout.

Relic straddled a newly placed rafter, waving them forward. He shinnied down the two-by-four, past two braces, to the top of the cinderblock wall of the new addition. Here, the building was but one story tall, raised above the level of the first floor of the old inn. He swung himself around the beam, grabbing the top of the wall, and stretched his legs down as far as they would go. He released his hold and fell a few feet to the concrete floor, rolling awkwardly over his pack. He stopped and raised a smile toward them, showing them a thumbs up.

Hailey climbed onto the rafter, a nursling monkey clinging to the wooden frame. She scooted stiffly down the edge, past each of the two braces, and to the top of the cinder blocks. There, she fumbled for a fresh grip, swung her legs off the tress and hung ungracefully for a moment. She put her hands on top of the wall, the lowest place that she could, and stretched downward.

She was thankful Relic did not tell her to jump – this was hard enough without someone pushing her to go faster.

She released her hold and flexed her knees as she struck the floor, rolling twice to an unceremonious finale.

By the time she'd stood, Ash had made a similar landing.

The rain had stopped but the sky remained black. Thunder growled at them again.

"This way." Relic trotted through an unfinished doorway and along the backside of the inn, away from the new addition and back toward the original section and the second story room where they'd been captive. Ash glanced at her and waved her forward. She was glad the giant of a man had fallen off the other side of the inn – they would not have to see him again now. And whoever came to the man's aid would be on the other side of the building, too. She tried to run but her legs seemed wholly incapable and the effort felt like a sack race with a drunk. She was well past caring, glad to know that she could move at all.

Relic reached the end of the inn. He peered carefully beyond it and raised a hand, motioning them to stop.

CHAPTER 35

Relic curled his finger then pointed up the slope to their left. She recognized the route – they would be heading for the little spring. She slowed to a fast but steady walk.

The clouds thinned and began to open. Sunshine angled low on the horizon, sneaking under the clouds, knife-like shadows stretched across the ground. The trail up to the spring was well packed, so although it was wet, the mud was thin. The inn was large enough that they could hear only fractured voices coming from the other side. They could keep the building between them and the men and get away unseen. Relic stayed a bit ahead of her, Ash bringing up the rear.

When they reached the spring, she noticed it was full, even though the pump continued to run. Relic patted the engine on his way past, a gesture of approval. What had he done?

Beyond the spring, Relic found a trail that led up-ward at an easy slope. Where were they going?

"Hey," she croaked, her voice dry.

He slowed and waited for her.

"Shouldn't we get back to Ash's truck?" She knew he kept his keys above the visor. "So we can get out of here?"

"Won't they be watching his truck, waiting for you?"

"Maybe. But the workers have all kinds of trucks parked there. They won't know which one belongs to him."

Ash came to a stop next to her.

"What do you think?" she asked Ash.

"We'd have to go past the inn. Past the guy who fell off. And who-knows-who-else out there, helping him." He rested his hands on his knees. "Right now, they'll be gathering around, looking for us pretty hard, everyone on high alert."

"Up to you," Relic said. "But there's a place up here a ways, an outcrop where we can dry out. And eat and rest."

"Water?" Ash straightened his back.

"Yep."

"I've got to drink." Ash nodded at Hailey.

"Well, you're welcome to come." Relic turned and started back up the trail.

Ash waited for her until she shrugged, the decision made. She was too tired to think about anything but plodding forward, anyway.

They shuffled along, the trail thinning as it steepened, and arrived at a small cairn, a stack of four rocks marking a turn in the trail. The switchback took them to the top of a plateau, level and broad. From here, another plateau rose a few miles away. She hoped to hell they were not going that far.

The inn and the river had disappeared beneath them and the setting sun had become harsh against her eyes. An unusual outcrop of rock rose from the flats, a thick ledge of sandstone over a smooth bed of sand the size of a small bedroom. Relic went to a rubble of stones on the other side, slid off his pack, and stretched.

She hobbled into the natural shelter and sat with her back to the smooth rock that curved upward into a roof above. Ash followed her, feet dragging, and sat a short distance away. They both lay back against the concave stone and rested.

"Hey, uh, any chance we could get some water?" Ash looked first at Relic, then at her.

"Yep." Relic walked behind a table-sized rock and returned with a large plastic water-cooler container.

"Where the hell did that come from?" She sat up. And what other kind of office equipment is this hermit squirreling away in the middle of nowhere?

"A gift." He set the water-cooler down and pulled a cloth rag out of its top. He rummaged through his pack and found an empty water bottle, which he filled from the big container. He put the lid back on the cooler and tossed the water bottle to Ash.

Ash handed it to Hailey and she drank nearly half of it in little time. She returned it to Ash, who emptied it.

Relic carried several stones to the center of the shelter and arranged them in a circle. Then he strode out across the plateau, wandering about.

"How can he keep walking?" she looked at Ash.

"Beats the hell out of me. Who is that guy, again?"

"His name is Relic. I think he's some kind of recluse or something, but he helped me get away from that giant." She pulled her knees to her chest and told him again about the old basement in the inn and being chased into the canyon north of where they were now.

She looked beyond their little camp. A native iridescence brewed in the eastern sky, opposite the sundown, lilac rays bouncing against a streak of watercolor clouds.

A chill ran through her and she shivered. Relic appeared at the entrance to their shelter, arms full of rough tinder. He dropped the wood by the ring of stones and left again. Soon, the light would be fully gone.

She was hungry and exhausted and dehydrated and wet and barely thinking at all, let alone thinking straight, when she saw what she would swear was a lone coyote, standing at the edge of their shelter, staring at her as if she were a squatter who'd hijacked its den.

CHAPTER 36

"Burke!" The man rasped over the phone, vocal cords tarred with years of cigarette smoke, mental state frayed with too much vodka.

"Yes?" Burke hated these calls from Tobias. Absolutely hated them.

"My man Odin is in the hospital?"

"Yes. He fell off the roof."

"What the hell?"

"He was after a couple of intruders. He chased them onto the roof just as a storm hit. The shingles were wet, really slick, and he slid off. Broke his left fibula and three ribs."

"And what of these intruders?"

"We're on their trail. They can't go far and we're searching the whole area. We'll get them."

Tobias was silent for a moment, not a good sign. Burke shifted his weight and stared at the ceiling in his office. The recent turn of events could ruin a lot of effort.

"I'm assigning Parker and Bashir to replace him. Tell Odin to get back to L.A. as soon as he's released from the hospital."

"Will do." He rolled his eyes.

"Put one of the new men in the place you call Demon's House, to keep watch there."

"Demon's Roost, yes."

"Give me three good reasons I shouldn't pull you and the whole enterprise, right now, have Parker and Bashir close up shop."

Burke fought against a reflux of stomach acid. He had to be careful here. Tobias was in charge of security and was influential, but he and Burke both answered to a higher boss. Tobias was not authorized to pull the operation on his own.

"We'll find the girl and her friend, for sure. They're in the desert, without food, water, transportation, anything. We have their cell phones, wallets, all their stuff. That's one. Second, I have things well in hand with the local authorities, a set up that's taken months to line up just right. That's a huge investment that's paying off. Third, the profits must be rolling in by now – we've taken five deliveries in just the last two weeks. This operation is worth twenty-five million a year. We can run this for months without a hitch and when our boss is ready, we all just walk away."

"I have my doubts, Burke. But Bashir will get me a full report after he arrives. He'll replace Odin and work under Mason. Parker will keep watch over Demon's Roost."

"Fine by me."

"Call me in four days. If you don't have the intruders by then, or if you're report doesn't match Bashir's precisely, or there are any more screw-ups, I'm taking this higher up."

Burke's patience was wearing thin. "Do what you need to, Tobias, but keep something in mind. You don't know all the factors, here. I've taken certain steps to protect this project, things the boss approved directly."

"Don't get too cocky, there, slick. My men will be watching you, too." Tobias hung up.

"Kiss my ass," Burke said to a silent phone.

CHAPTER 37

"Well, look who's joined us," Relic said as he strode into their make-shift camp. He rolled more wood onto the pile and knelt to the ground, petting the dog that Hailey had fed earlier in the day. The dog responded to Relic like a puppy, licking his hand, rolling onto the dirt for a tummy rub.

"Holy crap. That dog followed us all the way up here?" Ash leaned forward.

"That hamburger was pretty tasty, I guess." She extended a hand to the dog, who hurried over, rubbing its fur against her leg, poking its nose into her ribs. "Whoa, it sure is friendly."

Relic moved to his pack and removed a bag of beef jerky. The dog stayed with her but sat up, its ears at full attention. Relic tossed it a piece and the dog lay down next to her, meat balanced on its forepaws, enjoying its meal.

"Is it a he or a she?" Ash asked.

"She." Relic handed jerky to Ash and Hailey.

The dog swallowed the last of her dried beef and sat up, staring at Hailey's food. She broke it in two and handed half to the dog, who made quick work of it. Relic dug a shallow spot in the sand and pulled a light rain jacket from his pack. He tucked it into the ground and poured water into the depression. The dog went quickly to the water and lapped it up.

"What are the odds she would follow us all the way here?" Hailey took her time with her share of the sweetened beef.

"What do we call her?" Ash chewed on his piece.

Relic added stones to the fire pit and stacked wood carefully inside. "What about calling her Chance?"

"Chance?" Ash asked.

"Yeah, I see it." Hailey swallowed. "She took a chance on us. We'll take a chance on her."

"Her first name could be Last," Relic grinned.

"Last Chance - that it shall be." Hailey rubbed the back of Chance's ears, soft as petals, and the dog leaned into it, encouraging more.

Relic reached into his pack and gave each of them, including Chance, another long piece of jerky. He took one for himself, pulled his hunting knife, and began shaving strips from one of the branches of firewood, getting past the rain-soaked outer bark. When he was done, he tossed a pack of matches to Hailey. He pointed to the wood, then stood and trotted back out into the open, searching the ground.

Hailey scooted closer to the fire ring and tried to light the shavings, without any luck. Relic reappeared with more wood and tossed it onto the stack. He crossed his feet then scissored down to the ground.

"Sorry," she offered him the matches, but he'd already pulled another pack from his pocket.

"Keep 'em." Relic struck one and cupped a hand around it for a moment, watching it catch. He lit the wooden slivers carefully and blew gently into them, the flames pulsing against his cheeks, deepening his eyes. The unsteady light grew, exaggerating his dangling goatee and long hair, a caveman, she thought, needing only a jaguar pelt on his shoulders or a string of giant claws around his neck.

She touched her tangled hair, feeling a bit like a cavewoman herself.

Relic reached into his pack and tossed a plastic flask to her like it was an old habit. She took a long pull on the homemade gin and handed it to Ash. He took a sip, his eyes opened wide, then he took another.

"I want to thank you." Ash handed the bottle back to Relic. "You saved our skin back at the hotel, and now this – food and water and…"

"…gin," Hailey added.

"No worries." Relic scooted away from the fire a bit, and they found themselves pulled into its twists and turns, its mesmerizing ebb and flow.

God, she was tired. Her butt felt like it was growing roots into the sandy soil and she was grateful for it – she'd never have to move again. Then she remembered to ask: "Did you find your way to that other canyon you mentioned? Hell's Roost or whatever it is?"

"Demon's Roost. Yep. There's a shallow trench dug in the bottom of the gorge. In there are metal drums, fifty-gallon size drums. None of that was there a few weeks ago, when the flash flood went through." His eyes narrowed. "The only thing you bury in fifty-gallon drums is something you never want to see the light of day – something dangerous."

"Like what?" Ash asked.

"Like something toxic. Maybe, I'm guessing, toxic waste."

"Damn." Hailey straightened her back.

"What are we going to do about all of this?" Ash drank from the water bottle.

"If we can get to your truck, we can get back to town and report it to the sheriff." Hailey motioned for Ash to hand her the water. "If we can trust him."

"What do you mean?" Relic asked.

"I told him about the killing, the cement grave and the big man, that giant of a man chasing me through the tunnel in the basement. He said he'd investigate but then, after we got here, we saw him leaving the hotel with Burke. He was patting the deputy on the shoulder, shaking hands like old friends. It didn't look like he was investigating anything."

Relic passed her the gin. "You can put this story into the papers, can't you?"

"I hope so."

"A reporter's job is to make injustice visible."

"Ash, can we trust Martineau, the editor?" She took another swig.

"Huh," he expelled a puff of air. "Martineau's a spineless old hog," Ash shook his head. "He's known for being in the pockets of the local leaders, businesses, and the city council. He's almost famous for it. It's a thing around here, you know?"

"It's a thing, huh?" She took another quick drink, her muscles beginning to warm.

"A what?" Relic asked.

"A thing," Ash replied, taking the flask from Hailey. "What's a thing?"

"The editor's reputation as a spineless, officious ass."

"Well, that's something…" Relic stared into the fire.

"It's a thing, you know…" Ash pressed the gin to his lips.

"No," Relic shook his head, "I guess I don't."

"You don't know what a thing is?" Hailey leaned back on her arms.

"It's usually a noun, right? A person, place, or thing…" Relic's voice was serious.

"Oh, right, well, yes, a thing is a person or an object…" Ash handed the moonshine back to Relic.

"That's what I thought…"

"But when we say something is a thing, it's not a noun type of thing, it's a thing type of thing, like a thing that's special, a thing that people know about." As she spoke, Chance rolled against Hailey's leg and began to snore.

"So, a thing can be a thing, a regular thing, and also a special thing, and that's when you call a thing a thing?"

"How long have you been out here, Relic?" Hailey tittered, the gin loosening her tongue.

"Not long enough, I guess," Relic smiled broadly, his teeth gleaming in the firelight.

"So, can we trust Martineau to publish our story?" Hailey asked.

"We can run it on the internet," Ash leaned forward. "Martineau doesn't know this, but I run a local blog. It competes with the newspaper, so…"

"A blog?" Relic passed the moonshine to Ash again.

"Don't ask," Hailey chortled.

"I withdraw my question."

"If Martineau won't publish it, we can." Ash spoke with confidence.

"Good to know. Now, what about the deputy?"

"Don't know what to tell you there. But once we're back in town, we can call the feds, too, to make sure the sheriff pays attention to it." Ash took another swallow of gin.

"So, what's the best way to get to Ash's truck?" She stroked Chance's fur, warmed by the fire.

"What about your Blazer?" Ash said.

"Those men have my keys, remember? Yours are above the visor in your truck."

"Oh, right…"

"Where is it?" Relic took the gin back from Ash and tucked it into a sleeve on his pack.

"By those house trailers, where the other vehicles are parked."

Relic ran his fingers through his goatee. "We can hike back north, past Bitterbrush Canyon, where we climbed out with the rope, back to the camp we used last night, then down to the road. From there, you have to go south again, along the road, to get to where all the cars and trucks are parked."

"Oh, man," she moaned. "How long would that take us?"

"If we run…"

"…no running…"

"…well, at a regular walk, it'll take most of the day to get to the camp we used before. Then another day to get to the road. You could hitch a ride into town, like you did before, or go back to the parking area by the trailers."

"What about that mountain bike trail? I took a bike ride over there," she pointed, "to the north. I went off the main trail for a while, close to the rim, but the trail must be east of us."

"You could, but it meanders all around. Unless you ran into someone, it would take you even more time to get back to town," Relic said.

"If only the man who tied us up hadn't taken our cell phones…" Ash complained.

"And my purse," she mused.

"That reminds me," Relic reached into his pocket

and handed her a bottle of clear nail polish.

"Where did you get this?"

"Must have fallen out of your stuff at the other camp."

She held it up to the light. "It's missing some."

"Yeah, I found a good use for it."

"Strengthening your toenails, Relic?" she smiled.

"Of course. And pouring some of it down the lock outside your hotel door. So the guys who put you there couldn't come storming in on us before we were up and away from there."

"Huh." She slid it into her pants pocket. This caveman may not know a "thing" when he sees it, but he knows how to re-purpose one.

"So, we need to go back the way we came, not to Bitterbrush Canyon," Ash's words began to slur, "and shlip past the bad guys at the inn, eh?"

"Yep. And there's another option, too. A quick side trip."

"Yes?"

"Demon's Roost is due south of here, not too far. We can get there without them seeing us and maybe go down into the canyon there and check it out."

"What's to see there?"

"Remember there are trucks going in there? Well,

they're taking in those fifty-gallon drums and who knows what else. I'd like us all to see it before you go to the sheriff, or the FBI, so you can report on that, too. Whatever they're doing here, you can bet what's happening at Demon's Roost is a key part of it."

"They took Ash's camera, remember? We can't take any pictures…"

"I can sketch what we shee." Ash waved a hand at them. "When we get home…"

Hailey nodded. "How much longer would it be than going straight to the inn and to Ash's truck?"

"Half-day, if it goes well."

"I'm up for it. You, Ash?"

"Shoore."

CHAPTER 38

They woke with the morning light, Ash a little more slowly than Hailey. Relic offered them each the last of his bread, flattened dinner rolls he'd had in his cargo pants for a day or two, but they wolfed them down with some satisfaction. He rationed them each a large handful of peanuts and M&M's, a mixture he assured them was the finest trail food known to man. He reserved the rest of the beef jerky for another time and they set out toward Demon's Roost in good spirits, expecting a quick look there and then a return to the inn, where they'd sneak along the river and back to Ash's truck and fresh food and hot showers.

They crossed the plateau for a couple of hours, following Relic along a narrow trail, of sorts, that led south along the rim to a tall jumble of red rock. They wound closer to the formation and down a gentle slope to more stones. When they made their way through those, the land changed dramatically, a narrow canyon opening below them like a pit rimmed in a sandstone maze. Relic put his binoculars to his eyes and scanned the bottom of the canyon, but it all seemed quiet, motionless.

Hailey could see a trench of sorts along the bottom, a wooden shed to the side, and a pickup truck parked near the edge of the excavation.

"There's the rock formation that gave this place its name," Relic pointed behind them.

A stack of dark red sandstone rose against the cool sky, flat and horizontal in the middle, sides rising along the edges. A straight-backed piece the shade of iron climbed the back, a primeval throne forged by an oven deep in the earth.

"Yeah. The Demon's Roost," Ash said.

"How far down do we want to go?" Hailey asked.

"If you're up for it, let's go a little closer." Relic let his binoculars dangle against his chest.

Ash looked at her. "Sure. I'd like to get a better view of that trench, maybe see what's in it."

She nodded.

Relic slid the pack off his back and leaned it against a rock. "I'll get this on the way back up." He grabbed a water bottle and tucked it into a shoulder sling. He hung that and his binoculars over his neck. He pulled a bag of trail mix from the pack and jammed it into one of his pants pockets then turned and smiled broadly at them, his goatee wagging in the breeze. The man was enjoying himself.

They walked down a series of switchbacks and eventually across a huge, flat stone with no trail or brush or marks, smooth as a polished gem. The massive rock billowed toward the canyon, its edge dipping out of sight on their right. She stayed as far to the left as she could.

When they stopped again, she was surprised at the progress they'd made. The hike was steep but the distance to the bottom of the canyon had been deceptive – it looked much farther away from just a short distance higher. Relic lifted the binoculars to his eyes.

"See anyone?" She asked.

"Quiet as a grave down there."

The shed seemed to be one of those pre-built models, one that's hauled to wherever you want it. A forklift sat to the side of the outbuilding. The tops of a couple of metal drums could now be seen lining the trench.

They resumed their trek and after a while they could see the path ahead levelling out near the end. Relic stopped to rest behind a chunk of stone the size of a four-wheeler. Hailey and Ash moved to the same rock and leaned against it. The shed was much closer now.

They were only a dozen feet higher than the floor of the canyon, which was remarkably level and free of rocks and debris. Whether that was natural or whether men had shaped it that way, she could not be sure.

"This'll make a good sketch, from this angle." Ash moved to the side, back up the canyon a few steps, and down again. "Hailey, take a good look too. Help me remember later."

"Sure."

"See the drums? Count them for me?"

"Ten. That I can see," she said.

"Me, too."

Hailey stared into the canyon. "I forgot how easy it was to just take a snapshot of something with a phone. Memorizing a scene is a little…well, I'm way out of practice."

"A good sketch will be perfect for your article, though." Ash waved at the site.

"Yes," Hailey smiled, appreciating the hunt for more information. "But let me get the right count on those drums…"

"What?"

"I'll just go over there and take the right count and come back…" she started moving away.

"If we see any dust rising along the road," Relic

pointed, "we'll give you a quick whistle."

CHAPTER 39

Hailey walked past the wooden shed. Attached to the outer shell was a plywood lean-to, of sorts, with wooden two-by-fours as posts – outdoor storage under some shade. It was too dark underneath to see much. She moved toward the pit of fifty-gallon drums.

A forklift sat a few yards away, a weathered beige, tines protruding like twin tongues, bare and shiny from use. Beyond that was a backhoe for clearing rock. Its jointed arm angled upward then sharply back to a tooth-lined shovel, its iron head napping on the ground. Three wooden pallets leaned against a rock near the side of the machine.

The trench was a few yards wide and much longer than that, most of it empty. A dirt ramp rose from the floor of the ditch to the level of the roadway. A silver, double-cab pickup truck sat sideways in the road, blocking the path down the ramp.

She wiped the sweat from her forehead and adjusted her shirt. She could feel the sun nearing its zenith, the swelter bearing down. The breeze had shifted, the air trapped in the canyon with them, recirculating the heat. Nature's convection oven.

Across the way, along one edge of the trench, rose a rectangular entrance, an open doorway straight into the cliffs. It took her a moment to realize it was not her imagination. A large pile of broken rock had been shoved to the left. She'd heard there'd been uranium mining in some of these canyons, years ago, but they'd all been blasted shut. This one had been excavated.

She jogged across the ground to the edge of the opening, five feet wide and maybe seven feet tall. There were no braces or frames or bricks to hold the walls or ceiling in place, but the sides of the carved-out tunnel were remarkably precise and even. Maybe the rock was stable enough that extra supports weren't needed.

She couldn't see Relic or Ash from this angle. No one seemed to be around, so she moved to the edge of the opening. A buzzing sound reached her ears but her mind, unable to place it, ignored it for a moment. Then she looked to the ground and saw the snake, wound tightly in a coil, just beneath a jumble of rock.

"Crap!" She leapt backward, her legs a springboard

into the air, then moved quickly away and into the tunnel until the sound finally stopped, the snake no longer rattling its warning.

She took a breath and turned into the dark, the cool air chilling her skin. An oil lamp sat on a neat pile of stone. She lifted the glass chimney. A burned-out wick drooped to the side, the body of the lamp empty, no more kerosene in it to burn. She replaced the chimney and put the lamp back into place.

She'd have to go into the mine with just the light from outside.

Her soles echoed against the close walls as she moved farther in. The tunnel turned gently to the left, deeper into the mine. A smaller shaft angled to the right. She looked behind her. The entrance had shrunk to the size of a picture frame, only a little ambient light reaching her now, and her mind seemed to close in against her as tightly as the cold rock walls. How much deeper did it go? Which branch of the tunnel should she take? Should she sprint back to the light and warmth and freedom?

Whatever was going on here, the secret might lay deeper in the mine.

She shuffled her feet along the ground and extended her arm to avoid bumping into the side of the wall. She moved past the branch to her right, staying in what felt like the main shaft. Though dark, she sensed something directly ahead of her, so she kept advancing until suddenly her toes struck something hard, a clang of metal against her shoe, and she stopped. Her arms lowered ahead of her until she felt the rounded end of a steel drum. She moved to her right and felt another one, then another, blocking the path farther into the tunnel.

The mine was filled with fifty-gallon drums.

She turned and looked behind her, but her sight was useless here. Black on black, the tunnel was as dark as the night sky, no stars, no moon, no hint of light, just an eerie, inky depth. She remembered her run through the basement of the old inn, her body a wraith flying through a wall of onyx.

She moved her hands in front of her eyes but saw nothing at all, as blind and isolated from the world as in hell itself, and her muscles twitched with a flash of panic. It's OK, she told herself, it's OK.

She heard a distant clatter, pebbles rolling from the walls of the mine.

Her heart skipped a beat.

She remembered the matches Relic had given her last night, so she pulled them out and struck one. The flash made her close her eyes for a moment. When the flame settled into the cardboard, she moved it close to the drums but found no writing or symbols on them. When it nearly burned her fingers, she flicked it out. The light had been reassuring but was not bright enough to help find her way out of the tunnel. She stood with her back to the metal drums.

She knew to walk straight away, directly opposite of where she stood, into the sightless black. Trust yourself.

Twenty long, lonely steps finally brought her toward a shade of coal-gray, a hint of daytime outlining the edge of the side tunnel she'd passed on the way in. She saw nothing in there and decided she'd had enough anyway. She was not going down that black tube, too. She rounded the curve, the light of the entrance now a postage stamp in the distance.

Without warning, rocks began clacking against each other and hard onto the ground, the tunnel suddenly alive and crumbling around her. She ran as fast as she dared, prancing her feet high with each stride, avoiding debris on the ground, arms outstretched toward the light.

CHAPTER 40

She skidded to a stop by the old oil lamp and put her hands on her knees, breath heaving. She listened for more sounds from within the mine but heard none. The walls must be unstable, she thought, but at least there was no one else in there with her. She hoped.

She moved slowly outside the mine, keeping to the side opposite where the snake had been, watching and listening for the deadly reptile. She walked out of the shade, to the edge of the trench, and counted twelve of the old oil drums, more than they could see from the trail. How many were behind her, in the old mine shaft? Was the trench a temporary place for the drums, until they moved them into the tunnel? What the hell was in them?

Across the entrance, a solid wall of rock rose like a skyscraper to a ragged swath of sky. She stood for a moment in the bottom of the belly of Demon's Roost, goose bumps rising despite the heat.

She looked back to find Relic and Ash standing casually by the rocks at the edge of the trail they'd taken to the bottom of the canyon.

Suddenly, movement caught her eye and she focused hard on it, a shadow under the lean-to by the shed, a human form sliding to the edge of the wooden post.

The man had a pistol in his hand.

She stood on her tiptoes and waved her arms in the air.

Relic and Ash stopped and stared at her a moment and she pointed frantically to the storehouse, too afraid to yell.

The man leapt from behind the shed and fired a shot toward Relic and Ash, the explosion beating against the high cliffs, vibrating down to her toes. Relic and Ash ducked out of sight and the man ran toward them, rapidly crossing the open ground.

She had to do something, and quickly.

The shed would be good cover and, as the man ran away from it, she crossed the trench and moved close to the lean-to along the side. She came under the plywood roof and let her eyes adjust to the shade. Three shovels rested against the wall and a cot lay next to them. The guard must have been napping earlier when she'd walked past. Two cans of gasoline were tucked by the wall, along with a small cooler.

She glanced at the backhoe. She lifted one of the gas cans – it was nearly full – and jogged to the machine. First, she dragged a pallet to the digger and soaked the wood with fuel. She glanced around but did not see the gunman, who must be beyond the other side of the shed. Then she began sloshing gasoline over the metal panels, the exoskeleton of a sleeping monster. She poured it onto the seat and controls, then over the digging arm as high as she could reach, then over the engine in back. When she was done, she tossed the empty can to the ground, pulled the matches Relic had given her at camp, and knelt close to the wheeled tracks.

The first match flickered out. The second one caught the fuel and air rushed around her with shocking speed, oxygen into a vacuum, the digger suddenly ablaze. White vapor billowed from the cab and dark smoke leaked from beneath the engine.

She stepped away, the heat blasting her like a solid force, shoving her back toward the shed.

Black smoke now roiled from the machine, a swirl-ing summer storm but toxic, concentrated. The monster wheezed, sizzling heat forcing air through the gaps in its metal skin, then it coughed in fits, electricity short-ing, the doomed engine trying to start. An oily, burning sheen soon engulfed the backhoe, a column of angry heat distorting the air and rising toward the cliffs.

"Time to go," she told herself, moving back to the shed, searching the path beyond.

Two more shots echoed against the canyon walls.

CHAPTER 41

Relic shoved Ash ahead as they fled up the narrow trail, heading for a rise as fast as they could move.

Boom!

A bullet ricocheted off the rock they'd been leaning against seconds earlier, its ring vibrating in his ears.

He let Ash pull ahead a few feet, staying on the path. Turns and curves around the boulders would lead to natural cover, even if only for a moment or two.

Boom!

He could hear footfalls behind him, the man running to reach the start of the upward trail. Ash slipped for a moment, his boots skating over loose scree, but he caught himself and rounded a chunk of sandstone on their right. Relic followed him and slid to a stop behind the rock.

"Keep going," he yelled to Ash, who seemed to take his words to heart, pounding the dirt as it steepened into another turn to their right, then left, out of Relic's view. He climbed atop a stone about four feet tall, above and behind the boulder he'd just passed.

The gunman had started up the trail, twenty yards from Relic, breathing hard into the chase. Relic dropped to the path again, legs pumping, rising into the turn, climbing again as the trail straightened for a distance. Ash had disappeared ahead of him.

Relic rounded another sharp, steep bend and there, to the right, were a jumble of boulders. He spun behind one, pulled his hunting knife from its sheath, and peeked over the top of the rocks.

The gunman labored up the path, slowing his pace. As he began to look up toward Relic, a strange sort of gasp burst from the canyon floor. Fire raged behind the man, flames consuming the digger, spreading across its back and high against its skeletal arm.

The man turned to see what had caused the sound. He stood anchored there, mesmerized. Leaden smoke churned from the innards of the backhoe, rising toward the top of the cliffs.

Relic stayed behind the rocks.

The gunman glanced toward where Relic hid then back to the burning machine, no doubt calculating what the fire meant and what he needed to do next. He must be wondering who lit it, who else was in the canyon, and how many of them there might be. And who might be waiting for him along the narrow trail. Slowly, cautiously, he walked back down the path, his head swiveling like a needle on a compass.

When the man seemed committed to returning to the bottom of the canyon, Relic slid from the rock and followed him, knife still drawn, looking for Hailey and hoping she was well hidden.

The gunman stopped at the rock at the bottom, searching for whoever else was there.

The backhoe began to roast red-hot, spitting and sparking into the dirt around it, smoke dense with grease and boiling paint. The man held his pistol at the ready, running toward the wooden outbuilding.

CHAPTER 42

Hailey slid against the back wall of the shed and inched toward the edge. She peeked out quickly and ducked back. The man with the gun was running toward the front of the storage unit. She listened as his pace slowed to a cautious walk. The sound of his boots on gravel came closer and closer to her hiding space. She focused on the ground in front of her, ready to run, when she saw a piece of wood near her feet, a two-by four-brace, about three feet long.

The thump of feet on the ground slowed as the man approached, then, it seemed, passed the front of the shed. She bent at the knees and lifted the board with both hands and peered around the corner. The man had indeed moved past, but she could not tell whether he was still heading toward the burning backhoe or circling the shed. She stood there, stock-still, fear shaking her fingers. She pressed harder against the two-by-four, firming her grip, and took a step around the side of the shed, closer to the trail that would lead her to Relic and Ash.

She stopped midway along the side of the structure and listened again as closely as she could. The fire continued to rage to her left, just out of sight, huffing and crackling. An acrid smell wafted through the air and her stomach clenched.

She took another step toward the front of the shed.

Her diversion had drawn the man back to the equipment, but she could not see Relic or Ash. They must still be running up the canyon trail, away from the guard.

She reached the edge of the outbuilding and stopped.

No sound came from nearby.

She tightened her right hand on the two-by-four then took her left hand from the board and wrapped her fingers along the edge of the shed, ready to propel herself forward and toward the trail to the top of Demon's Roost. Just as she bent her knees to run, a hairy arm reached around the corner, pinning her wrist. The shock of it sent a jolt through her backbone and she leapt and screeched, the jab of adrenaline an electrical charge through her muscles. The man spun around the corner, a crooked grin on his dirty face, his hand now tightening against her fingers, crushing them together: a handshake meant to break bones.

She raised the board in her right hand and swung with her body weight, bending at the knees, the pine-wood crashing against his shoulder with all she could muster. Something seemed to snap within him, his face suddenly contorted, eyes squeezed shut, and he yelped like a wolf pup, releasing his grip and stumbling back.

Hailey dropped the two-by-four, panic sending her fully into flight and she pounded across the flats to the rock that marked the trail to the top, expecting a bullet in the back at any moment now, any moment. She grabbed the big stone with her hands, slinging her body around the corner, amazed the bullet hadn't come, and continued up the slope as fast as her tired legs could carry her.

When she reached a large rock on her right, she powered around, spinning to see behind her.

Her muscles were burning, her lungs heaving, and she leaned against the rock for some respite.

The man had left the shed, pistol still in hand, but one arm was cradled in the other. He moved past the smoldering backhoe and toward the truck at the end of the trench.

Her breathing slowed to a more regular series of gasps.

The man walked past the trench, slid into the

pickup, and sat there for a moment. The truck rumbled to a start.

She stared at the funnel of smoke rising from the backhoe, astonished at everything she'd just done.

CHAPTER 43

Mason entered Burke's office just as a barrage of static crackled over the radio. Mason went straight to the CB on top of the bookcase and grabbed the microphone.

"…there?"

"We hear you," Mason replied, his eyes downcast, concentrating on the transmission.

"We just got punked." It was Parker's voice, the young man posted in Demon's Roost, and he was agitated, angry.

"What happened?"

"Three people, two guys and a girl, showed up somehow, from the top of the canyon. They surprised me and attacked me, and they lit the backhoe on fire!"

Burke stood from his chair, backbone stiff.

"Did you get them?" Mason asked, grinding his teeth.

"No. They ran back up the trail toward the top."

"You're in the truck?"

"Yeah, to get to the radio and get you a report."

Mason tightened his grip on the microphone. Burke shook his head in frustration.

"Get your ass after them! Now!"

"Can you send some help? The backhoe's burning like a coal from hell."

Mason looked up at Burke but kept speaking. "If that's the case, it's a lost cause. We can't get anyone there for at least twenty minutes. And those assholes will be long gone by then."

Burke pounded his fist on his desk. It had to be that reporter, Hailey.

"We don't have the time or the manpower to send guys to help you right now. You've got a pistol – use it if you have to, but catch those bastards," Mason snapped.

"Yes, sir." The radio clicked off on the other end.

"Damn it." Mason slapped down the microphone. "Who the hell are these people?"

Burke spoke tentatively, knowing this was Mason's turf. "You might want to alert everyone. Check the security around the inn again."

Mason's cheeks flushed and he nearly shouted again but turned and stomped out of the office.

Burke stared blankly at the wall behind the radio

and plopped back into his chair. If they kept it up, this Hailey girl, the photographer, and the mystery man were going to screw up his plans entirely. His best guess was that they would come back to the inn again – they had to come this way to get back to town. And there was one way to sneak past the inn.

It was time to join Mason's men on patrol.

CHAPTER 44

Hailey plodded up the incline and past the rock where she, Relic, and Ash had rested when they'd first come down the trail. Several desk-sized rocks were piled together at a turn in the path and she stopped to sit and rest.

The silver pickup truck was still sitting on the other side of the shallow trench, beyond the entrance to the old mine. She could just see some white smoke from the tailpipe, so she knew the engine was still running. Why hadn't he left to report what had happened? Or to get more help?

She remembered how that hairy arm had grabbed onto hers, tight as a pair of vice grips, and her muscles twitched. He'd nearly had her. Really had her. She patted her hands on her knees. If she hadn't grabbed that piece of two-by-four...

Footsteps slid across the gravel and she turned to

see Relic and Ash coming toward her.

"Are you OK?" Ash touched his hand to her shoulder, and she welcomed the connection.

"Yeah. You guys?"

Ash nodded.

"I heard gunfire."

"He's a lousy shot." Ash's lips rose in a crooked grin.

Relic handed her the water bottle. She drank deeply then set it in front of her. "See that pile of rubble down there, next to the trench?" she pointed.

"Yes," Ash nodded.

"Just in front of that, out of view from here, is an old mine shaft."

"Really?" Ash wrinkled his nose. "There were uranium mines out here in the 1950s but they've all been blasted closed, for safety. To keep people out."

"Well, this one's wide open. I went right in – pretty deep, too."

"They're not safe. They're not stable."

"I noticed…"

"That's what all that debris is, then." Ash nodded toward it. "It used to seal up the mine."

"Did you find anything?" Relic asked.

"More of those fifty-gallon drums. Deep inside, enough that the light from outside can't reach them. I don't know how deep the drums really go because the ones I found blocked the way."

"They're using the old mine to hide the barrels," Ash said.

"Yeah. And they have plenty more space before the main shaft is full. And there's a side tunnel, too." She handed the water back to Relic.

"Nice diversion." Ash pointed to the smoldering backhoe.

"Yeah, but that guy is still down there, just sitting in that truck."

Relic put the binoculars to his eyes.

"What's he doing?" Ash squinted into the distance.

"He's talking into something with a wire attached. Must be a radio, maybe a citizen's band." Relic adjusted the lenses.

"Oh," Hailey sat straighter. "Burke had a CB radio set in his office."

"Shit on a shingle," Relic lowered the binoculars.

"Yeah, so he must be talking to the others." She nodded.

"And now, he's coming this way," Relic pointed.

CHAPTER 45

"Daylight's wasting," Relic waved them back up the trail toward the top of the canyon.

Hailey stood and Ash let her take the lead, running, if she could call it that, as fast as her tired legs could go. The path rose steeply for a bit, then became a series of switchbacks. They were in and out of view, if the man below was looking, and their lead was dwindling. She kept her focus on her feet, careful to avoid loose rock as the climb steepened even more. The way levelled suddenly, her pace quickening over even ground before she reached another chunk of sandstone.

She glanced behind her. Ash was close. Relic was farther behind, watching with his binoculars.

She searched the slope for signs of the guard who'd left the truck. This time, he was not likely to give up – there would be no more diversions down by the backhoe.

Ash reached her and turned to look below. Relic

had started back up the path. They lost sight of the guard now and then as he wound his way along the route leading up the canyon.

Boom!

She jumped at the sound of the pistol. The man was shooting from some distance, but Relic was in the open, running toward them.

Boom!

Relic slid to a stop behind the rock with her and Ash.

"What do we do?" Ash's eyes had tightened into slits.

"We keep going, of course," Hailey said.

"Look," Relic pointed farther up the trail. "It opens up there for a long stretch. If that guy catches us there, he'll have a wide open shot at us."

They moved quickly to the spot where the route crossed atop a solid, rounded wall of rock. The view to their left dropped out of sight. Ahead, the path was exposed – there were no twists or boulders to hide behind. They would have to get to the other side before the guard reached the place where they stood now.

"He's too close." Relic's words were matter of fact.

Hailey patted her thighs with her hands. "What, then?"

"We have to keep going but lower, down below the

trail. Out of sight." Relic moved quickly away, exploring over rocks and beyond the ledge.

"Here…" Relic waved them forward, but they were already close behind him.

Rocks had tumbled into place from higher up the canyon, scattering across an area about ten yards in front of them. Beyond that was the massive, single stone they'd walked on top of earlier in the day, the open stretch of trail. The same rock, nearly vertical down here, looked impassable. Still, Relic did not hesitate. He led them along, pebbles and fist-sized rocks sliding under their feet, rolling downward with every step. The slope continued all the way to the canyon floor, an angle so steep that if they'd started down, it would not allow them back up. They reached the end of the scree and came to the side of the cliff below the path.

"He can't see us down here. Once we cross, we'll be past that flat, open area and back into some cover."

She stared at the rugged slope of sandstone, its vertical wall falling over two hundred feet below them. She wished Relic had brought his pack down with him – his climbing rope was old, but she knew it would still hold. They could have anchored it above and tied into it to cross the barren cliff.

Maybe they could go down the slope to the canyon

floor again and hide among the rocks there, maybe make their way to the road and back to the inn. They needed to get to Ash's vehicle so they could get back to town for help. Before she could voice her thoughts, Relic had begun a horizontal climb across the bluff.

Shit. She knew she was going to have to make the same traverse.

The distance was only about forty feet across. It was the vertical height that terrified her.

She watched as Relic reached up for fingerholds, placing the toes of his boots against cracks and bumps in the stone. Damn it. He made it look easy. In minutes, he'd made the crossing and stood on a boulder angled into the slope. From there, it looked like a manageable climb back up to the path that could take them to the Demon's Roost formation and out of the canyon.

"Hailey, you go next," Relic said.

Shit. Shit. Shit.

Ash gave her a look of encouragement. "Focus on the rock in front of you and take your time. Test each hand and foothold then move on to the next."

"You do this for fun, don't you?"

"Not today," his lips pressed firmly together. "You can do this, Hailey. Just stay focused. Don't rush yourself, especially near the end."

She stared at the cliff face.

"Don't stop until you're done and don't hurry in the meantime." Ash offered her his hand to help with her first move.

"Good advice." She knew she was stalling.

"First good foothold there," Ash pointed.

She had no more options, so she put her right hand in Ash's and her left foot onto a rough spot on the cliff, a couple of feet from where she stood. She released her hold on Ash, launching herself onto the rock, grabbing with her left hand, searching the slick stone for a grip with her right.

She rested there for a moment, her face inches from the rock, and stole a breath.

A faint ledge appeared in her periphery, jutting a couple of inches from the rest of the cliff, so she shuffled toward it. Thank god her shoes hadn't given out yet. A new handhold was more illusory but she pressed her fingers against a slope on the wall and moved her weight onto the ledge. She wiggled her right foot until it, too, rested on the same feature. She slid her feet farther along the ledge until it disappeared. A crook in the rock rose on her left. She got a solid grasp on it and searched for another foothold.

Though small, she continued to find cracks and

bumps and rough spots where she could get a grip and inched steadily along until she saw Relic standing on a rock on the slope and the thought of reaching him made her gush with hope. Her right shoe slid suddenly from its perch, the shift straining her hold with the other foot, and she dug her fingers as tightly as she could against the bluff, her right leg dangling in the air below her. She searched in vain for another spot for her foot, shifting precariously.

She couldn't stay here for long.

She glanced at Relic again, who encouraged her forward.

"Use your hand holds for the last bit." He pointed at the wall.

She willed herself not to look down but then she did it anyway, damn it, the air between her and the bottom of the precipice spiraling her head like a launch into space.

She brought her eyes back to the rough surface in front of her face and tried to steady herself.

Using her hands, she scooted farther along and found another grip. Then her left foot slipped abruptly from its perch and she fell against the rock, her cheek smashing into the sandstone, and she was dangling by her fingertips, both legs fully extended toward the abyss, her heart pounding like it would be the last thing she would ever feel in this life.

CHAPTER 46

"Here!" Relic had moved across the cliff face a step, swinging the harness he used for his water bottle. "Grab hold!"

The nylon strap swung close to her face, agonizingly close, then back and downward, impossible to reach, but then it rose up again, toward her left hand. She felt her right hand slipping slowly away from the rock and when the harness reached her this time, she grabbed it with her left and held with all her strength. Her other hand fell away from the rock and she pivoted downward in a rush until the strap swung her roughly into the scree below where Relic held. She grabbed the strap with her right hand, too, and cycled her feet against the steep incline, panic driving her breath until she found a solid stone and she wrapped an arm around it.

She was still panting when Relic stretched a hand to her and asked if she was all right. What an absolutely insane question.

The rock she'd gotten hold of seemed stable and, as she realized that, she worked to slow her breathing and get her thoughts to focus again. After a moment, she reached for Relic and let him pull her onto firmer ground.

"Stay in the boulders and head that way." He pointed. "You should intersect with the trail in a short while."

She glanced at Ash, who had started across, but when she looked below him, her stomach seemed to drop to the canyon floor in a weightless spiral. She turned away from the bluff and stepped cautiously across the scree, placing her hands on rocks before each move on the unstable slope. Eventually, she reached a less dangerous spot and recognized the narrow path – she could see their footprints from earlier. She pulled herself onto the level ground and lay down, the earth reeling out of control, the ground as jiggly as jello in an earthquake. She rolled over and wretched.

She rose onto her hands and knees and stayed there, holding steady, taking shallow but measured breaths until she could turn and sit onto the ground. She heard the clack of boots on stone, Relic and Ash making their way across the slope and toward the trail. She wiped her mouth and tried to collect herself.

Relic came toward her, the water bottle and its harness back across his shoulders with his binoculars. Ash stepped up next, placing his fists on his hips and looking about, a man atop a mountain, momentarily confident. He turned and ran to her.

"You're OK?"

She nodded, not yet trusting her voice.

"We're past the exposed part," Relic spoke in a low voice. "But we lost some time and the guy is still coming up. He'll be at the start of the open space pretty soon now." He lay his binoculars back against his chest. "So we'd best get going."

Ash helped her to stand. "Can we shake this guy?" he asked Relic.

"Don't know. But the path peters out up here, the closer we get to the top. If we hide our footprints, he might lose the trail and slow down. He won't know if we're planning an ambush, or if we've circled behind him, or if we're just long gone." Relic ran his fingers through his goatee, thinking.

"Or?" Hailey asked.

"We might have to actually ambush him if he keeps on coming." Relic turned and motioned them to start back up the trail.

Hailey and Ash shared a look of concern.

She began to walk up the route to the top, trudging forward, until she heard the now familiar sound of a high-pitched buzz, a tiny snare drum beating beneath the stone in front of her.

CHAPTER 47

Hailey held her arms straight out, shoulder length, a signal to stop moving and listen. The snake was dead ahead of her under the shade of a rock, staring at her, waiting for her next move.

She heard Relic and Ash stop behind her.

She moved her left foot back slowly, slowly, then shifted her weight onto that leg and raised her right foot ever so smoothly, quietly backward until she'd moved a safer distance away.

"Take another step back," Relic whispered.

She made another very slow move away.

"Finding this rattler is a stroke of luck," Relic said.

"What?" Ash said, trying to keep his voice low.

"We're trapped now, between the snake and the man with the gun!" Hailey forced the words through her teeth.

"Here…" Relic had picked up a stick, about four

feet long, a wrinkled old branch, and moved in front of Ash and Hailey. He slid his feet gradually closer to the angry serpent. He leaned forward, holding the piece of wood in the air, then plunged it onto the ground directly in front of the snake.

In a flash, the rattler struck at the cane, spinning it nearly out of Relic's hand and he gripped it tighter and pounded it into the dirt again and the snake struck with such speed and accuracy it made them all jump and marvel at the sight all at once. A third time, Relic poked the stick toward the ground in front of the snake and it lurched forward but more slowly now, its fangs opened wide, something sticky in its mouth, it seemed. Relic plunged the branch into the ground a fourth time, but the rattler slithered without striking, its fury dissipating.

"He's tiring out," Relic whispered as he circled the snake, climbing the ground behind its hiding spot. He leaned over, jabbing the stick right next to the snake's head but, again, the serpent watched it without striking. Relic squatted close behind the reptile now, balancing on the branch, and just as he moved the wood again, the snake eyeing it cautiously, his hand snapped quickly to the back of its head, grasping it tightly. It hissed, angry again, but caught now, writhing under Relic's hold of it. He dropped the stick and grabbed the body with his other hand, letting it wrap around him, holding the head immobile.

Hailey and Ash stared at the spectacle.

Relic had captured the rattlesnake and now held the deadly animal in his hands.

"This is the solution," he said, no longer whispering. "Comin' through…"

They stood quickly aside, happy to let Relic take the snake down the path and away from them. He turned back and said, "hide over there." He motioned with his head to some large rocks farther up the trail. Then, he moved to a tall stone at the end of the open part of the path and squatted low, waiting.

Hailey scurried up the trail and behind a chair-sized rock. Ash followed and they peeked over it, watching closely.

The guard had reached the open path and was moving quickly toward them, toward where Relic hid. The man was young and lanky, with close-cropped hair and eyes pulled tight with intensity. When he reached the rockier terrain, he slowed and looked carefully ahead of him, pistol pointed at the sky, ready to aim quickly in any direction. He stepped closer and closer to Relic.

Relic leapt up, tossing the snake fully into the man's face. He screamed, dropping his gun, flailing and spinning, falling to his hands and knees then popping back up, arms waving in the air, raw fear in his eyes and he fled from the deadly serpent, groaning in shock.

Relic snatched up the pistol and waited.

The man backed away quickly. The snake slithered across the ground, curving and sliding with a speed that seemed impossible without legs. Soon, it was into the shelter of rocks and out of sight.

The man continued to step backward along the open trail, his mouth a circle of surprise and awe. He finally stopped and stared at Relic.

Relic raised the pistol and aimed it at the guard.

The man spun and ran fast and low for cover at the opposite edge of the opening. Relic waited until he'd nearly reached the boulders.

Boom!

Relic fired a shot into the air.

The man panicked again, twisting past the rocks, pounding down the trail as fast as his legs could carry him.

CHAPTER 48

Exhausted as they were, the incident with the snake and the guard had reenergized them, and they congratulated Relic on his quick thinking and new-found talent as a snake handler. He'd explained that the key was wearing out the rattler so it could be caught and, of course, keeping careful hold of its head. Still, Hailey knew it was a risky move.

They stopped frequently to look back down the path, but the guard was long gone. Although they'd expected reinforcements to enter the canyon down below, they saw no rising dust or other signs that had happened. Maybe they were stretched thin, with no more men to spare at that moment.

As it turned out, Relic had fired the last bullet in the six-shooter. Hailey assumed the guard had more ammunition, but of course it was no use to him without the pistol. Even if he had decided to turn around, and somehow managed to catch up with them, the guard would be unarmed and at a distinct disadvantage against the three of them. Rather than carry the empty gun with them, Relic wiped his fingerprints off and tucked it between some rocks. He piled nearly a dozen stones into a cairn nearby so the police could find it later, then they kept on climbing. The quiet below helped them all to relax, moving at a steady but leisurely pace.

By the time they reached the rocky seat of Demon's Roost, the sun was casting shadows sideways. Relic picked up his pack and they trekked across a more gentle incline, eventually reaching above the canyon walls.

Hailey walked slowly as she scanned the wide terrain. Ridges and mesas rose across the horizon, layered in sunset shades of plum and seafoam, the sky turned upside down it seemed, as if they were suddenly walking under water. She stopped to gape. The guys were waiting up ahead, as lost in the view as she.

They took nearly another hour to return to the camp they'd used the night before. They had neither the daylight nor the energy to return to the road by the inn – their original plan to get back to town and seek help. They would have to try that tomorrow. For now, Hailey wanted only to sit in one place and put some food in her stomach. Even another piece of toughened jerky.

When they reached the overhang, Relic quickly re-built the rock pit and gathered more wood for the evening. She'd felt light-headed and a throb in her temples that Relic said was dehydration. She and Ash drank an entire bottle of water each, refilling it from the "water-cooler" Relic had stashed by the little camp.

"You're pretty good at starting fires." Relic smiled and pointed to the pile of sticks in the firepit.

"Got any gasoline up here?" She clucked, pulling the matches from her pocket. She organized the wood, placing the smallest sticks and some grass at the bottom and larger pieces above. After six matches, the seventh one took hold, the newborn flame expanding slowly. She found the exercise enthralling, even a little therapeutic, as her success grew into a steady flame.

The sun finally set behind them, the eastern sky fading from violet into the dense ink of night. A lone star appeared above blackened cliffs.

Relic handed them two pieces of barbeque jerky each. They sat and chewed on the dry beef, passing the water bottle around as they ate, three Neanderthals masticating their daily protein. She half expected Chance to show up for another meal.

"I'm still amazed at what you did with that snake," Ash said to Relic.

"That evil thing had us trapped," Hailey added.

"Respectfully," Relic looked at her, "the snake is powerful, but not evil. We presented a danger to him, as much as he did to us."

"Well, I guess that's true…" she stared into the campfire.

"Every creature faces its own challenges in life. I'm grateful to the snake for helping us get past one of ours today."

"I hadn't thought of it that way."

They sat quietly for a while and Ash began to nod, still chewing on his jerky. "I was just thinking about that rainstorm, earlier, and crossing that old rooftop. I got to wondering again what happened to that big guy, the one who fell off when he was chasing us." He spoke between bites.

"You know," Hailey said, "I think he's the one Burke called Odin. I'd forgotten about that, but I think that's his name."

"The god-king of Norse mythology?" Ash asked, motioning for Relic to pass the water bottle.

"Yeah. Scary thug."

"He's named after a king?" Relic asked, pondering the fact. "That gorilla gives a whole new meaning to the phrase 'governing body.'"

Ash and Hailey chuckled.

"Yeah, give some people an inch and they think they're a ruler."

They laughed at the old joke.

A branch in the fire cracked, a small explosion of sparks popping outside the fire ring.

Ash interlocked his fingers and watched the smoke blend into the night. "You can really feel this place, can't you? It's like a living, breathing, thing."

Relic smiled. "Scientists have recently found a thumping in the earth, all the way around the planet…"

Ash looked at him.

"…every twenty-six seconds."

"Everywhere?" He patted the ground next to him.

"Yep. Everywhere. They think the epicenter is somewhere in the Atlantic Ocean."

"What is it?"

"Seismic activity of some sort."

"But a regular thump? Every twenty-six seconds?" Hailey asked.

"Myself, I like to think of it like a heartbeat," Relic said.

"Heartbeat…" she said into the air, wondering if it was more than a metaphor.

"Hey, I meant to ask you, Relic – what does the

word 'sakwa' mean?"

"Blue. Blue Spring."

Ash nodded.

"Blue? That's so different from all the other names around here," Hailey tucked her hair behind her ears. "I've seen them here and there on the maps. Places like Demon's Roost, Hell Roaring Canyon, Devil's Tail…"

"That's because sakwa is a Pueblo word. Native names for these places don't have the same fixation on hell and damnation."

Ash stood and excused himself. They listened to him scraping through the sage brush, clumping against rocks he couldn't see.

"Hand me your shoes." Relic extended his hand toward her feet.

"My shoes?"

"Yes. They need some repair."

She slid one off and examined it in the light of the fire. The leather top had chaffed raw, gouges crisscrossing the once smooth surface like claw marks. Stitches that used to hold the top of the shoe to the sole had stretched apart near the arches. Too much more and the leather would loosen altogether.

Relic took the footwear and shook it out. He pulled something from his pack and wrapped it around the splitting shoe, ripping the end with his teeth. He finished pushing the wrap onto the leather and handed it back to her.

"Won't last long, but maybe long enough."

Duct tape encircled the shoe near the arch, holding top to bottom.

"The sole is nearly broken," she mused.

"Just broken in, is all." He smiled.

She handed him her other shoe. "I'm feeling a little broken in myself."

"Still angry?" he asked.

She knew what he meant – he was asking about her mother. "Always."

"Remember that people are shaped by what they think. Wait too long, anger can fester. Don't let anger turn to bitterness."

"That's easy to say…" She heard the frustration in her own voice.

"Generalize it. Turn it into anger at injustice brought by others. Or at something broader, something you care about. And then go do something about it, whatever you can. Keep taking positive action, like you did today. After a while, the resentment gets crowded out, easier to chuck away."

She nodded.

"We can't control everything about ourselves," he shook his head, "obviously. But with practice, we can guide our thoughts. Don't let others walk through your mind with muddy feet. And don't put any mud in there yourself."

She stared at the shoe in her hand.

"Take Sakwa Spring. We can't just go fix it directly, but we can allow it to heal itself. Let yourself heal up, too. Taking action on something important will help. You're on that path now, taking positive action, filling your mind with that. Keep going…"

His words felt like a warm pat on her back. "Thank you." She'd been pining for times past, resenting their loss. Wondering what her mom would think of all of this, wishing she could call her and tell her about this trek into the desert. But despite the tales from science fiction, no one can travel back in time. All you can do is revive your determination going forward.

A waft of smoke blew into her eyes, disrupting her thoughts. Ash fumbled back into camp, Chance trotting at his heels. "Look who dropped by for supper." Ash plopped into the sand. The dog hurried to Hailey for some attention.

"It's not fair—you're her favorite." Ash winked at her.

"Did she smell the fire?" Hailey asked.

"Or the succulent beef jerky?" Ash grinned.

"Well, she's persistent." Hailey rubbed behind the dog's ears.

Relic pulled a piece of dried meat from his pack and tossed it to Chance, who finished it in four quick bites. He passed the flask of gin to Ash. "Not much left – may as well finish it off."

Ash took a drink then Hailey took her turn, the liquid fire warming her belly. Ash stretched his legs in front of him and leaned his elbow onto the ground. Chance gave him a turn to pet her head.

Hailey felt the urge to move, so she slipped her duct-taped shoes onto her feet. She eased herself upright and walked into the night, stiff-legged from the day's climb.

Firelight cast weird shadows on the rocks and sage, blades of light shifting across the ground, swaying her like a boat on choppy water. She shuffled toward a desk-sized rock lit weakly by the night sky. Feeling the top of the sandstone block, she moved to the far side and found a place to sit. She'd never seen so many stars, pin pricks of light scattered across the void. She recognized the big dipper and felt some comfort from its boxy pattern, a beacon reminding her which planet she was on.

Anger. Resentment. Bitterness. All the same kind

of poison, she thought, progressing on a destructive course. You can't drink the poison and expect someone else to die.

She thought of Chance, her fuzzy ears and lolling tongue, and it made her smile. Why is it so much easier sometimes to connect with a living being from an entirely different species than to connect with one from your own? All creatures have their own struggles, even a rattlesnake. And all creatures share the universe. Maybe we are all spirits, each having their own experience, but all with a similar energy, all sons and daughters of the same planet, birthing and dying right here, right next to each other. Maybe canines just understand that a little better than primates.

A good life is always long enough, whether it's human, or hound, or otherwise. Channel your anger into something that is just and fair. Turn it into something positive. Taking action is the way to turn it into something worthwhile.

She determined to write an exposé on all of it – everything going on at Broken Inn – whether Martineau, the editor, or the sheriff, or anyone else wanted her to or not. She was not going to let the injustice stay invisible.

CHAPTER 49

Tufts of grass shivered in the morning breeze, honeyed with the glow of sunrise. What had been invisible last night was risen from the darkness now, radiating shades of almond and olive. Cups of deep red flowers perched atop a patch of cacti, arching upward, dreaming of the next rain. A tiny whiptail lizard stood on a rock nearby and moved his narrow body up, down, up, down, his morning pushups. Hailey wondered what his world was like, what challenges he would face – the falcon, the snake, maybe, and his own hunt for food. How different his life must be from hers, yet how much the same.

Chance had helped keep her and Ash warm in the night, huddled between them. Her mouth curled in a subtle smile now, an innocent, sleeping baby with an incongruous set of sharp, canine teeth.

Hailey sat up and tucked her legs beneath her. Relic had left his place by the firepit. She filled her lungs with the cool morning air.

Chance lifted her head, ears revolving mechanically, fuzzy radar dishes on a swivel. Hailey rubbed the fur on Chance's head, triggering a brisk wag of the tail. They were in the same pack now, the four of them. The dog stood and trotted into the sage.

Relic walked back into their camp and knelt by the fire ring. He grabbed a rag and lifted a small aluminum pot from the coals.

"Coffee?"

"Sure."

"We'll have to share my mug." He poured a stout looking liquid into an insulated cup and handed it to her.

"Straight up this morning." She lifted it in a mock toast to him. The mug had a logo on its side with letters. "What is NOLS?"

"National Outdoor Leadership School."

"Oh." She put the cup to her lips and sipped, the taste a mixture of overcooked coffee and river mud. Tough medicine. Not a salted caramel macchiato with whipped cream, but welcome, nonetheless. She took a longer swallow and handed the mug back to Relic.

Ash began to stir, emitting a low groan.

"All I have is trail food for breakfast." Relic handed her a baggie filled with peanuts and M&Ms.

"Oh!" The M&M's had melted in the desert sun, chocolate and peanuts clumped together like models of molecular carbon, without the sticks in between. She broke a chunk apart, tossed a couple more peanuts in for more protein, and chewed on the mixture with a smile.

They took their time, watching the shadows shrink, letting the air warm into the day. Ash ate his share from the baggie. Relic told them to drink all the water they could. Hailey helped Relic bury the ashes from their fire and scatter the fire rocks. Leave no trace.

Ash rubbed his eye with the back of his hand. "So, what's the plan for today?"

Relic smoothed a patch of sand in front of him. "Here's where we are." He drew in the ground with a stick. "We go back down to the spring. Just beyond is a bit of a rim, above the inn. We can look around from there and try to spot the security guards. If you go straight down, maybe curve a little away from the inn, you get to the gravel road, the one that runs up and down the river. To the left is Demon's Roost. To the right and back up the slope a bit is the inn. Go straight and you come to the river. There's a bank above the river, maybe six feet high. Stay close to that. The inn is mostly hidden from sight as you follow the river upstream. You should be able to go all the way past the inn to the trailers and to your truck without being seen."

"I still wonder what happened to that big guy, the man who chased us on the roof," Hailey said.

"That's quite a fall…" Ash shook his head.

"If he's out of action, that leaves maybe two more guards, the one at the inn and the one that was in Demon's Roost. Plus that other guy." Relic erased his map in the sand.

"Burke."

"Right."

"I don't trust him, but he didn't have a gun or other weapon that I could see. When I interviewed him, at least."

Ash nodded. "Then getting past the inn should be a good plan. It's the fastest way to my truck. Then we hightail it to the sheriff and call the FBI."

"There will be workers, carpenters and brick layers and all, moving back and forth, at the inn and at those trailers. They're good guys, just here for the job. If you run into any of them and they ask you what you're doing, you could say you're looking for Manny."

"Who's Manny?"

"Met him the other day. He supervises the project. I did some work for him and he got me supper. He's also the one who got me the water-cooler water we've been drinking."

Hailey's brow rose. "You did some work for these guys?"

"Why – is that a 'thing'?" Relic grinned.

Hailey squinted and lowered her head, a mock disapproval.

"Well, the giant nearly caught me below the spring," Relic continued, "and Manny happened along and got me out of it. Had to haul cinder blocks for a while, but it got me out of trouble and got me food and water, to boot. Manny's a good guy."

"Got it." She tightened her lips.

Chance sat at the perimeter of their little camp, waiting patiently for them to depart. They stood, dusted themselves off, and the dog took point, trotting ahead of them as if she knew where they were going, glancing behind to make sure they were following her lead.

They trekked across the lower plateau and down the narrow game trail they'd used the day before. By mid-morning, they'd reached the switchbacks that brought them to more level ground just above the spring. A gasoline engine puttered near the water and when they approached the pool, they could see that the water was down again.

"Shitheads." Relic put his hands on his hips.

She and Ash came up behind him and stared at the spring, precious water being sucked up and regurgitated through the mechanical pump. Cattails drooped along the edges and a sheen of something bad coated the surface of the water that remained.

"One guy can be pretty stupid all by himself, but nothing beats teamwork for some genuine, certified stupidity."

"Stupid, or evil?" Ash asked.

"Same thing, if you judge by the results," Relic said.

Hailey watched the concern on Relic's face. "What are you thinking?"

"This will require a more permanent solution." Relic motioned toward the motor. "But first…" he waved them forward. They walked slowly along the dirt road to a place where it turned downhill toward the inn. A rusted bulldozer stared at them across the way, lined up, it seemed, for more serious damage to the little spring.

No one was around. She noticed that Chance had disappeared. Probably looking for her next free meal.

Relic lowered to the ground and duck-walked to the edge of the ridge that dropped below and paralleled the back side of the inn. He slid out of his pack and lowered into the dirt. He rummaged through a pocket on the pack, pulled out his binoculars, and began to scan the area below. She and Ash lay down beside him.

"There's a truck on the road, there," Relic pointed, "south of the inn, on the way to Demon's Roost, with its hood up. Must be broken down, but there's nobody around there at the moment."

"I see it," Ash said.

"It looks clear right now. If you go straight to the truck, you'll be pretty close to the river. Just keep going and you'll drop below the low ridge that runs along the water. From there, it should be pretty safe. When you get to the trailers and the parking area, keep an eye out, but there will be others walking around, so you shouldn't be really obvious."

"And take off from there," Ash nodded.

"It's a plan," Hailey said.

"Until it's not." Relic tucked his binoculars away. "So be ready to improvise if you have to."

"Where will you be?"

"Up here for a bit."

"Wait – what are you going to do?" Hailey asked.

"Just a little harmless fun." He beamed, a kid at the carnival. "I'll keep an eye on you until you get to the river. Then I've got some work to do here."

"Yes?" she asked.

"I'll figure it out. But you guys get to town and

bring back some help."

"Go now?" she asked. "Just like that?"

"Just like that. Unless you want to hike back up the plateau for a couple of days."

She and Ash looked at each other for a moment. "OK. Thanks for everything, Relic. We really owe you."

"On that point, let's keep any references to me as vague as you can, eh?"

"Got it." She stood and began a brisk walk down the road, staying to the far side of the inn, Ash scrambling to catch up with her. They had a plan, at least. Until, as Relic had said, they didn't.

CHAPTER 50

Deputy Dawson sat in front of the computer screen, tapping his finger on the desk. He'd called the FBI supervisor's office again for more detail, a fruitless quest, it seemed. The supervisor couldn't find the time to return his calls. The office clerk was sympathetic, saying he'd ask if he could send Dawson something from the files, but he'd made no promises. Dawson had been checking the secure email system every half-hour or so that morning.

Sheriff Glasser lumbered up behind him. "Got anything interesting?"

"No." Dawson turned, accidentally flipping a pen from his fingers and onto the floor. He watched it roll away but kept his head between the sheriff and the screen.

"Not wasting your time with that Broken Inn crap, are you? That's for the feds now, and well above your pay grade…"

"Just a quick check."

The sheriff clucked his tongue and shook his head, a round of disapproval. He was a bulging man in a uniform too tight for his age and weight. Round, blue eyes peered behind wire-rimmed spectacles as thick as hand-blown glass. His thinning hair was seldom combed, his shirt perpetually wrinkled. His generous waist carried a wide, brown belt with an assortment of keys and radio gear, wires running to a unit on his shoulder. The man seldom spoke highly of anyone, but Dawson had long ago chalked it up to a disagreeable disposition, a permanent condition.

"Take car number two and make a run out to Rattlesnake Hills and back. It's good to show our presence out there."

The Hills was a trailer park east of town, a place heavy with poverty and beer and depression. The deputies did their best to keep the meth labs from moving in.

"Yes, sir."

The sheriff wandered into the conference room, where another deputy sat watching a training video.

Dawson reached to log off the computer when something marked "FBI confidential" appeared among the emails, a spark of hope. He opened an attachment and scrolled through.

"Damn…" Names, sentences, and even whole paragraphs had been redacted from the file. "What bullshit," he said to himself.

Then he noticed something at the bottom of the file, a blacked-out photograph with a couple of words underneath, something that cooled his blood like dry ice.

He could get to Rattlesnake Hills, but only after a detour to the Broken Inn.

CHAPTER 51

Hailey kept her eyes on the old inn, heart pumping faster than it should, searching the doors and windows for any human movement. She and Ash were about fifty yards away, walking the dirt road that led from the spring and down toward the gravel route that ran between the hotel and the river. They passed an old Dodge truck on the other side of the lane. They made their way level with the edge of the building and, as they passed the corner, they could see men with shovels and wheelbarrows working near the porte cochère.

She and Ash were out in the open, but halfway there.

"That stalled truck is just ahead." Ash pointed his chin toward the vehicle, a quarter-ton with its hood angled upward, a bright, yellow parrot raising its beak for a bit of food. Canvas tarps covered cargo on the bed of the truck.

They hustled more quickly now, almost at a run,

the truck, a place to hide, close at hand. Twenty feet away, Hailey broke into a sprint, skidding to a stop in front of the wide, front grill, ducking out of view of the inn. Ash bumbled into her, crashing them to their knees by the front tire.

"Oh…"

"Uh, sorry."

She stood slowly and slid to the side of the truck, brushing her pants, watching the inn through the passenger and rear windows.

"Looks clear," Ash announced.

They moved past the edge of the cab and to the end of the bed for a better view. The walls on the new addition looked complete, and a crane or a tall backhoe of some sort was parked on the northeast corner, lifting tresses into place along the cinder block walls. She remembered shimmying down one of the new tresses in the storm, after the giant had slid off the old part of the roof. She took a breath, relaxing a bit.

They stared across the way at the construction project, men moving in and out of sight.

"Somebody's going to come back for this truck, to get it running again," Ash said.

"Right. Maybe we should…"

"Hailey!" Burke's voice sent a shock through her

system, a surge of fear tugging the back of her eyes, her lungs suddenly gasping for air and she spun, fist out, striking the man square on his cheek. He spun away from the blow, hand to his face, bent at the waist, and Ash stepped in, hands clenched, pounding Burke's stomach once, then again. Burke went down to the ground, arms covering his head, knees tucked into his gut.

Burke lifted his arms. "Stop, stop, will you?"

She stared down at him, panting, and glanced around. No one else appeared to be near them. "What the hell? What the hell are you doing?" She could hear a wheeze in her voice.

Ash backed a step away. "Who is this?"

"Burke. The guy I interviewed. The guy in charge of this whole project."

"No, not completely." Burke sat, legs straight on the ground in front of him. He lifted his hands. "Give me a minute." He wiped his mouth and worked his jaw. "I came to tell you—"

"What?" A nervous anger mounted with the pulse of her heart.

"I'm not here to hurt you. I'm not who you think I am." Burke took a breath. "Can I stand up?"

"No." Ash spoke through his teeth, his jaw set.

"OK, OK. First of all, I'm not in charge here. I

work the business end of this, the hospitality part of it."

"We're not exactly feeling welcome here." She opened and closed her fists.

"I'm not in control of the security. Those guys and I work for the same organization, but they do their own thing. They don't answer to me."

Hailey straightened. "So, what?"

"Well, here's the kicker. I didn't want to tell you this, but I see now I'm going to have to." He looked around, making sure no one else was near them. "I'm undercover, investigating organized crime out of L.A. I've been in this position for months now, getting close to figuring out how to bring these guys down."

"Bullshit." She put her hands on her hips.

Ash nodded an agreement.

"I'm undercover FBI. Special assignment. You can ask Deputy Dawson. He's confirmed it. He's cooperating with the investigation. I've been watching for you today. I figured you'd have to cross the road here sooner or later..."

"I don't believe you."

"Well, hell, I can't help you unless you do." He tucked his legs underneath him. "I'm going to forget what just happened here, but if you hit me again, you'll be committing a federal offense." He held his hands toward them, a gesture that was part defense, part supplication.

Ash and Hailey looked at each other and stepped away from Burke.

"We didn't just beat on an FBI agent that easy." Ash's accusation hung in the air.

"My goal is not to hurt you. And to be honest, you took me by surprise." He stood unhurriedly and dusted himself off. "Look, no weapons." He raised his arms and spun a full circle. "I'm telling you I'm undercover. Why would I help you if I weren't?"

"You haven't helped us yet," Ash said.

"Yeah, well there's a guard making his way along the river right now and he'll see or hear us any minute. If that happens, it's going to get out of control."

Hailey stepped away from the truck, peering along the low ridge paralleling the river. She watched for a moment and just when she was about to accuse Burke of lying again, a man's head bobbed into view, maybe a quarter of a mile away.

"Shit," she hissed through her teeth and backed away from the ridge. Ash stared at her and she nodded. Their plan to run along the riverbank to Ash's truck had just collapsed.

"Let's all walk calmly away from this truck, toward the hotel. If I can get you into a room there to hide, we can call the deputy and my supervisor and get some help. Or slip you away with some of the workers."

Ash's gaze moved behind her and he stiffened. "Hailey. It looks like the mechanics are on their way."

"Time to go, folks." Burke began to walk across the gravel road and toward the Broken Inn.

She turned to see a pickup truck in the distance, barreling toward them, dust spinning behind it like a sideways tornado.

CHAPTER 52

Ash scurried behind Burke, waving Hailey to hurry along. Workers by the porte cochère had stopped what they were doing and had begun to walk toward the trailers downslope, toward the river. Maybe it was time for a lunch break. She could use one of those herself.

Burke did not bother looking behind him, but she was sure he knew they were in tow. He marched through the glass doors, through the lobby, and into a partially finished meeting room. Unpainted drywall hid the framing, strips of plaster filling the joints where the wallboard came together. Canvas drop cloths lay crumpled in one corner. Used chairs lined against one wall, specks of plaster dotting their plastic seats.

"I've got an idea. There's a truck parked off the end of the building I use to drive around the site." He circled a finger in the air. "I'll get the keys from my office and take you to the truck and you can drive on out of here."

He turned and left the room in a rush.

"A ride out of here." Ash touched her arm, excitement in his eyes.

"Yeah, it's just…"

They waited for a moment, silence settling on them like dust.

"Here!" Burke leaned through the open door, dangling a set of keys on his fingers. "Let's go."

Ash followed and Hailey felt the pull of it, a chance to escape the place, and ran behind him. They travelled past the entrance to the cellar, the one she'd gone through to find the odd stuff down there, the one where the giant had chased her. Soon they were hurrying through the old part of the inn, a lonely, empty corridor toward a door on the end that looked like it had been twisted as a prop for a cheap horror movie. She glanced up the stairway that led to the room where she and Ash had been held captive two days ago, and she felt a quick shiver.

Burke stopped briefly to peek outside, then moved across a span of ground toward the dirt road that led to the spring above the ridge. A red Dodge pickup rested on the other side of the drive, the one they'd passed on their way down. She looked right and left, saw no one nearby, and followed him, glad to be out of the creepy hallway. Some distance away, the yellow truck that needed a repair was moving now, rolling toward Demon's Roost. The truck that had carried someone to repair the vehicle had turned back, upriver. Soon, both were out of sight.

They labored up to the dirt road and hurried to the Dodge on the other side. All three stopped to catch their breath, sheltered behind the pickup.

"That's better." Burke stood, moved to the end of the empty truck bed, and looked around.

Hailey leaned against the truck, muscles quivering from fatigue.

"Yeah." Ash looked at Hailey, his eyes tired but hopeful. He took a step toward Burke.

Burke spun toward Ash, arm outstretched, striking his head hard and fast, Ash turning from the blow and falling to the ground in a heap, a deep groan escaping him like smoke after an explosion.

Hailey leapt back from Ash and Burke, not believing her eyes for a second, then raising her fists in anger.

Burke held a six-shooter toward her chest, its silver chambers armed with bullets the color of dark copper. She realized he'd gotten the gun from his office when he'd gotten keys to the pickup truck.

"Oh, god." She dropped her arms and knelt next to Ash, pulling his hair away from his face, feeling his neck for a pulse.

"Bastard!" she yelled at him with all her might, forcing the air from her lungs, heaving for breath at the effort. "Why? Why are you doing this?"

"I tried to get you to leave us alone…"

"You told us you were an undercover cop! You told the *deputy* you were an undercover cop!"

"I did."

"Why?"

"I didn't really want to have to shoot you. I just wanted you all to leave us to our work."

She felt the blood flowing through Ash's carotid artery. He was unconscious, but alive. "So, wait…who did you kill and bury in cement?"

"The actual undercover agent. He pretended to be a security grunt here. That's what gave me the idea, really. He looked a little like me – not as handsome of course, but the same build and all. When the deputy checks with the FBI, they'll confirm there's an undercover operation here and the locals will leave us alone. I know how the guy sent his reports to the FBI, so I've kept that going. But you…" he waved the pistol at her and Ash, "…keep showing up and, well, the security goons here have a lot less patience with interlopers. Once they captured you, that was it. But then you got away and now…" his arms widened, a gesture of inevitability.

Ash groaned and pulled his knees to his stomach.

"You're first. Turn around, Hailey."

She could not will herself to move. "You're going to kill us? Now?"

"Now's a great time. No one around. I'll put you in the back of the truck and bury you with the rest of the waste."

"That's it, isn't it? You're burying toxic waste in the next canyon down, right? The old inn, restoring it and all of that, it's just a cover for what's really happening, isn't it?" She stared up at him.

His lips rose in self-satisfaction, a cheater's grin.

"Oh…"

"Turn around or don't, it's your choice." He straightened his arm, aiming the pistol at the top of her nose, and pulled the hammer back.

CHAPTER 53

A well-worn, yellow bulldozer rested along the dirt road, aimed directly at the little spring. Relic could see no one around, but the intent of whoever had parked the monster here was clear – Sakwa Spring was going to be forever wiped away, the grass and cattails leveled, rocks pushed aside, petroglyph cracked into dust. They were going to stick a pipe down its throat, pave paradise, and, as the old song goes, put up a parking lot.

Not if he had anything to say about it.

A pair of cables linked the body of the machine to each of the upper arms, hydraulic actuators leading to the large, iron bucket. The engine was behind the cab, a rusted exhaust pipe jutting straight into the air. Iron tracks, like those of a tank, were worn and caked with dried mud.

He ran to the cab and pulled himself up on the arm of the rearview mirror. Inside, the control panel was worn but simple: three dials, a set of keys dangling from the ignition, and one button. Two levers rose in front of the driver's seat. He'd have to guess which one did what.

He hopped into the seat and turned the key. The engine coughed to life, shaking the ground, vibrating his teeth. He pushed the right stick forward and the blade lifted a little from the dirt. He pushed on the left stick and the dozer jerked forward, rolling quickly down the road, heading for the edge of the spring. He tugged the stick to the left and the machine turned, away from the oasis and toward the engine pumping water from the pool.

So far, so good.

He eased the stick farther left, then right, getting a better feel for how to direct the machine. He pushed the right lever forward, lowering the blade closer to the ground, and jacked up the speed. The dozer closed rapidly on the water pump, scooping it into its iron jaw. Hoses popped under pressure, water sprayed into the air, and he could see the engine rolling sideways into the bucket on the dozer, spilling its gasoline.

Whoosh.

The pump lit on fire, fresh fuel on the broiling engine, now pumping only air through its ruined tubes, shaking, smoking, gasping to a final stop while the flames spread quickly across the greasy frame.

He turned the dozer farther away from the spring, following the water pipe toward the ridge and the framing that led to the water tower beyond. He aimed the dozer at the elevated cistern and made sure the accelerator was as far forward as it would go. The machine dug into the ground with earnest, speed rising as it crunched along the ground. He glanced to his left at the churning, metal track and gauged his next move.

He slid off the seat and planted his feet on the edge of the cab, hands gripping tightly along the sides and he counted, one, two, three…

He leapt from the dozer, clearing the churning teeth of the metal tracks as they propelled the machine closer and closer to the edge. He rolled to a stop in the dirt and looked up.

The dozer still held the ruined water pump in the cup of its bucket, black, oily smoke billowing through the open cab.

The yellow monster vibrated the ground as it rolled, a tank aimed at the ridge, its nose high and forward, unstoppable. It ran across the water line, shattering the pipe, following it off the edge of the ridge and downward, down to the base of the framing that held the pipe high in its arms. The wood supports cracked and splintered at the attack, popping like firecrackers, collapsing on top of the dozer as it plowed through, breaking the pine supports as easily as toothpicks.

The dozer gained speed as the slope steepened, hurtling like a yellow locomotive toward the base of the water tower and it hit with a series of explosions, the legs of the tower cracking and buckling until the dozer slid on its side, its momentum slowed but not completely stopped. The bowl atop the frame wobbled then swayed, the water inside increasing its momentum until a wave carried beyond its balance and the cistern tipped all the way over, reaching, falling toward the old inn in what seemed like a slow-motion movie, its sides splitting as it fell, water crashing against the rock and dirt like an ocean storm. In one, awful moment, the whole of the water tower, pipes, planks, posts, and boards, all of it exploded downward and into the weathered side of the old inn, near the part Relic had explored before, washing all of it into rubble.

CHAPTER 54

Dawson moved carefully under the porte cochère, earning inquisitive glances from some of the workers. He figured he'd check on Burke unannounced and have a serious chat.

He entered the new lobby for the old inn, shiny marble-like counters to his left, an open breakfast room directly in front of him. He walked to the right and stopped outside Burke's office, listening for any sounds within.

The floor creaked behind him and, as he started to turn, the cold barrel of a pistol pushed against the bottom of his skull.

Damn it.

His muscles seized tight and he instinctively raised his hands into the air. Fingers reached to his side and removed his police revolver.

"Hold still." The voice behind him was firm,

experienced.

"I'm here to see Mr. Burke." Dawson didn't really expect the statement to make any difference, but he was out of other options.

"He's not seeing you today. We're going to turn around together. Go slowly to your left and I will stay behind you. Got it?"

Dawson nodded. He pivoted to his left and felt the barrel again, in the center of his back this time, prompting him forward.

They walked stiffly into the empty lobby and then to their right, down the main hallway into the hotel. The doors on the first two rooms looked new but they were soon beyond them and moving down a dark hall toward a lone door and window at the end, some cheap, western prop with a deadly twist.

"Here," the voice directed.

Dawson stopped midway down the hall. The man behind him jangled some keys and opened the nearest room.

"Back up."

The deputy took two steps back.

"Now, into the room."

Dawson crossed the threshold. "You're making a big mistake."

The man pushed his pistol hard against his waist, forcing him farther inside.

Dawson figured this was really it – the time he'd dreaded and expected all his career, the closing moments of his life. He stopped for a final breath when something outside the room gathered speed, enormous, buffoonish, the sound of crumpling paper, it seemed, rolling toward them, crunching, shaking the ground. When it crashed into the wall, he spun, pushing the pistol aside as it fired, jabbing the gunman in the neck with his fingers and it was all over in a second, the man on his knees gasping for breath. Dawson stood there for a moment, drywall crumbling around him, plaster propelling across the room, a wooden post jutting from the ceiling.

He slid his service revolver and the gunman's pistol out of reach then handcuffed the man in a quick, well-practiced, move.

CHAPTER 55

Burke blinked at the thundering sound behind him. He took two cautious strides backward and peered around the tailgate. Hailey could hear wood splitting at the seams, the ground vibrating like a minor earthquake, but the truck hid the source of the noise from her.

He turned back to her, surprise on his face, then a steaming resolve. He took a careful aim again and she couldn't look, she just couldn't, and she squeezed her eyes shut, praying for relief, praying for her mother, telling herself she would soon be with her, and just when she knew it was all over, a snarl rose from behind Burke and Hailey's eyes popped open.

Chance lunged at Burke's ankle and bit through the muscle, teeth on gristle and bone. She could hear the grind of it, and he raised his arms to the sky, firing the pistol, surprise and anguish twisting his mouth in a knot of lips, teeth, and saliva.

The dog began to shake Burke's leg back and forth, fighting her prey, forcing her fangs deeper into his flesh. He wheeled around, flailing, spinning down to the ground with a thud. Chance lowered her head and stared at him, growling, digging her teeth deeper with every struggle he made to shake her off.

He'd dropped the pistol.

Hailey crawled to the gun and lifted it from the dirt. She blew the sand away and raised it toward Burke's stomach. He was blinded with pain, writhing in the dust, trying to kick Chance away with his other foot but the dog was too limber, twisting her body away, inflicting more damage each time he tried to pull free.

"Chance!"

The dog stopped to listen.

"Chance, let him go." Hailey stood slowly, using the front tire to help her up. "Come on, now, Chance, it's OK now. Good girl. Good girl."

Chance kept her jaw clamped tight, ears back against her neck, snarling. Burke curled into his belly and groaned, his hands on the temples of his head.

Ash rolled onto his stomach and slid his hands under his chest. "Ohh…"

"Ash…" She aimed the pistol into the air and helped him stand. "Are you OK?"

"No." He moved his head gently back and forth, working to focus.

"Chance! Here, girl!"

The dog's ears lifted and her bite relaxed, but Burke remained curled, in considerable pain.

"Come here." Hailey held out her left hand and knelt to the ground again. Chance looked at Hailey, then at Burke, then at Hailey again and finally let loose. She scurried to Hailey, tail high and proud behind her.

"You saved my life, girl." Hailey petted then hugged Chance around her shoulder.

Ash stood and leaned against the truck. "What?"

"Chance just bit on Burke here. Saved our butts." Hailey smiled.

"No shit?"

"No shit."

"Hey, Hailey, let's say we get the key from Burke here and hit the road."

"Great idea." She stood again and moved toward Burke, gun in her hand.

Burke had grabbed his ankle and was squeezing it, rocking back and forth. "Help me, I'll bleed to death…"

"You'll be fine," Hailey told him. His right pants leg was wet with blood below the knee, but it looked more painful than deadly. "Just keep holding it."

Ash moved gingerly, reaching into Burke's pocket. He pulled out a set of keys and stepped away.

Hailey kept the pistol on Burke, though he seemed wholly preoccupied with staunching the flow of blood. "Why don't you guys get into the truck first," she told Ash.

Ash slid across the seat to the passenger side and called for Chance to jump in. The dog hesitated for a moment then leapt in easily.

"Let's go get some help." Ash lay his elbow on the edge of the door, against the window.

Hailey stepped toward the cab and turned to climb in, but the sight of Mason stopped her cold.

He stood on the other side of the truck and laid a pistol of his own on the hood, aimed at Hailey. "I don't think the cavalry is going to rescue you this time."

CHAPTER 56

Water flowed along the back of the inn toward the cinder block wall of the new addition, pushing dirt and boards and debris ahead of it. Relic passed the dozer, now sideways in the sand, lifeless as a downed buffalo at the spot where the tower had been. Its engine had stopped cold, but the pump in the dozer's bucket continued to smolder. He slid down the slope at an angle, following the path of the water, making his way to the bottom.

He reached the level of the inn and watched as the flood spread across the ground to his left, searching out the lowest spots along the foundation, its energy slowly dissipating.

He looked along the outer wall of the inn. A white and yellow backhoe rested at the far end of the addition, its tracks looking more like a snow machine than a tank, its high arms capped with muscled levers, a narrow bucket with three giant teeth drooped from its single arm. He ran parallel with the wall and through an inch of water. When he reached the edge of the inn, man-made sounds floated toward him, shouts and footfalls, concerned and hurried. He rounded the wall and moved around the backhoe, watching workers coming toward him. He recognized Manny among the first of them.

Three men jogged between the backhoe and the corner of the new addition, pointing then running toward the old section of the inn. Studs and boards were splintered and jumbled along the outer wall, a mess of chopsticks, Jenga blocks, and mud.

"Hey." Relic waved to Manny.

Manny's eyes widened but he nodded and came toward Relic. "What is happening?"

"Little accident with the bulldozer." Relic nodded toward the tangled lumber and smashed-in wall half-way down the building.

"Holy…"

"Can I talk to you a minute?" Relic whispered urgently.

"*¿Que?*"

"Can you operate this machine?" he pointed to the backhoe. The workers had been using it to lift the awkward tresses into place on the cinder block walls.

"Roberto can," he pointed behind him.

"I have to tell you what's going on here and ask for a bit of help…"

CHAPTER 57

"Not the cavalry, you jerk – the Indians." Hailey nodded behind Mason, her lips rising in a smile.

A row of seven men, shovels and hammers in hand, had begun to march up the road toward the truck, more falling in behind them. Mason swung his head to see them, glanced toward Hailey again, then back to the crew of carpenters, masons, and roofers, their long, black hair and weathered skin looking all the world like warriors ready for battle.

Chance barked at Mason, the window keeping her at bay. Ash whispered to her and petted her head, calming her to a nervous whine.

"Put your gun down." Hailey took careful aim, her resolve surprising her.

Mason glanced between her and the oncoming men.

"When they get here, they'll beat the crap out of you, unless you surrender." They were in a stand-off, but

Hailey had a group of men who would not tolerate the likes of Burke and Mason.

"Screw it." Mason laid the pistol on the hood of the truck and raised his hands.

A man the others called Manny took charge of the group, shouting in mixed Spanish and English for them to tie up Mason. Hailey moved around the open door, sliding the gun she'd gotten from Burke under the seat.

Just then, Deputy Dawson emerged from the front of the old inn, one of the security guards in handcuffs. The deputy looked toward the trailer houses then toward Hailey, Ash, and Chance.

"We're going to go see the deputy over there…" Hailey spoke to Manny and pointed at Dawson. Manny nodded.

She hopped into the truck, closed the door, and started the engine. She drove in first gear down the track toward the inn, careful not to alarm Dawson. When they drew close enough, she parked and turned off the truck. Dawson watched as the three of them left the cab, Chance looking at Hailey and dancing around her feet.

"Hailey." Dawson's greeting was warm.

"Officer."

"Deputy," he corrected.

"Yes, deputy, you probably know Ash. He works

for the paper."

Dawson nodded. "Stand right there," he said to his prisoner, who obeyed. "Sherriff's on his way," he said to Hailey.

Boom!

They turned in unison toward the hardened sound.

From this angle, it looked like a white backhoe was raising its toothy bucket into the air.

Boom!

The percussion shocked the ground, a cannon firing into bedrock.

"Let's go," Dawson grabbed his prisoner by the cuffs and hurried him forward. Hailey, Ash, and Chance ran ahead of them.

Boom!

They sprinted across the open ground, climbing as it rose a few feet to the level of the inn.

Boom!

They rounded the new addition and stopped short, watching the backhoe as it lifted a corner of concrete and flipped it over, bending the rebar that reinforced it.

She and Ash looked at each other, unsure what to say.

Dawson moved behind them.

The machine jabbed its teeth under another part

of the concrete floor and groaned as it lifted the piece upwards, then over, onto the rest of the slab. There, on the underside of the chunk of cement, they could see the back and head of a human body, its dark hair matted flat, its lifeless form inert.

The body she'd seen buried days ago.

She flinched at the feel of Dawson's hand on her shoulder. "That's the man you saw?"

"Yes. Well, I would think so."

"He's Colby, an undercover FBI agent," Dawson said.

"You knew?" she asked.

"Just figured it out."

Hailey rubbed her hand against her neck. "Burke told us *he* was an undercover agent, just now, just a few minutes ago…but he was lying."

Ash glanced at Dawson and back to Hailey.

She took a breath. "Burke killed the agent, then pretended to be him."

"Why would he do that?" Ash asked.

"Because Burke found out the agent was undercover, and he assumed his identity so he could keep the sheriff away."

Dawson nodded. "Burke gave me an FBI contact card. He must have found it and realized Colby was undercover."

"How did you know?" Ash asked the deputy.

"I got an FBI file with Colby's description: height, weight, race, and eye color."

They looked at Dawson.

"Colby's eyes are blue. Burke's eyes are brown."

CHAPTER 58

"Deputy…" she began.

"Yes?"

"Burke's gun is in the truck we drove up in. On the floor, under the front seat."

Dawson's brow rose.

"And those guys, construction guys, down the road. They have one of the guards from here. He pulled a gun on us, but…they saved the day. They have him and probably Burke, too."

"Where?"

She pointed up the road, past the old part of the Inn.

Dawson stepped back for a better view.

Sirens wailed in the distance.

"Oh, and something else." She put her hand on Dawson's arm. "The next canyon down from here, Demon's Roost, there's a trench there with something buried, we don't know what, but it includes a bunch of fifty-gallon metal drums. And the old mine is full of them."

"Metal drums?"

"They're hiding them, so whatever is in them is not good. In fact, we've seen some hazmat suits. We're thinking," she glanced at Ash, who nodded, "toxic waste."

Dawson's back straightened. "The FBI file had a 'copy to' notice on it, to copy memos to both the environmental crimes and the organized crime units."

"The mob?"

"It's not that simple these days, but..." he shook his head once, "...sort of."

"What's the deal?"

"Proper disposal of toxic waste is expensive. There's big money in making it disappear, even at a fraction of the cost of legitimate disposal."

"Shit." Ash forced the air from his lips.

"These guys are a plague," Hailey hissed.

"And apparently the Broken Inn is their cover." Dawson pointed at the cinder block walls. "A so-called legitimate business with a reason for construction trucks going in and out all day long. If they used the old mine, all they'd have to do is seal it up again, the way the government did a few years back. No one would ever check in there again."

They stood there for a moment, thinking about

all of it.

"What's up with the smoke, on the other side of the inn?" the deputy asked.

Hailey glanced at Ash and spoke quickly. "We heard a big crash back there, but…"

"You didn't see who did that?"

She shrugged.

Two sheriff's vehicles skidded to a stop in the dust.

Dawson waved the deputies toward him but looked at Hailey and Ash. "You guys," he said, "see me first thing tomorrow morning, OK?"

"They took our wallets and phones," Ash said.

"And my purse…"

"Check with us tomorrow and we'll get 'em back to you," Dawson replied.

"Not too early…" Ash offered.

"Not too early, OK. Take a shower, first, will you? Or two or three of them." He released a quick grin and turned toward the arriving deputies. He shoved his prisoner forward. Now the man in charge, Dawson began instructing the other officers what to do next.

CHAPTER 59

Hailey and Ash wandered to one of the other deputies, who was handing out bottled water, an important courtesy in the desert. Ash took one and chatted with the officer.

Hailey saw herself in the side-view mirror. Dark hair hung from her scalp like the ends were dripping wet, tangled impossibly along the sides, a twig snagged near the bottom of the skein. Red dust burrowed into every nook and cranny, it seemed, along the curve of her nostrils, deep into creases across her forehead and down her neck. God, she thought, what three days of sweat and heat could do to a girl. Even Relic looked better than she did, and he lived among the caves and cliffs all the time. She ran her fingers through her hair, a brief attempt to calm the storm.

Ash was dusty and worn, looking tired but comfortable under the stubble on his cheeks.

"Can I get two extra, for a friend who's up the road?" she asked. The deputy handed her three bottles of water and moved toward some of the work crew.

They turned and walked past the old red Dodge and up the dirt road that ran in front of the inn. They followed it higher as it turned to the left then stopped to stare at the damage to the water tower and the back of the building. Water had soaked into the hill and along the outer wall of the hotel, staining the soil dark, like shadows out of place. The hole in the roof was still showing, the one Relic had lifted them through the night of the downpour. The cistern and tower had been reduced to rubble, scrambled into leaves of sheet metal. Pipes and two-by-fours aimed down the slope and into the inn, stuck like spears chucked into the side of a beast. The bulldozer had slid onto its side. Men climbed along the wreck, shoveling dirt onto a smoldering lump still pocketed in the bucket.

"Relic's doing, I assume." Ash pointed.

"No doubt." They shuffled higher along the road until they reached the top and walked to the little spring. They sat together on a rock at the edge. Though the soil had shifted in places and the cattails still looked sickly, water had refilled the oasis.

Chance trotted across the open ground and sat

next to Hailey.

"Hey, girl." She rubbed behind the dog's ears.

"That dog has adopted you." Ash said.

"It's mutual."

"What will your landlord say?"

"We're a package deal. If we need to, we'll sleep under the stars."

"We've no food for you now." Ash leaned toward the dog.

"I'm starving."

"I know a great place for Mexican food, in town." Ash's eyes shimmered, something tender there, and her breath caught for a moment.

"Deal." She felt like Medusa herself, snakes rising from her hair. Anyone who'd offer her a meal right now deserved to be knighted. "As long as we feed Chance first."

"Of course."

"I got these for Relic." She lifted the bottles of water.

"We should come back in a couple of days, leave him some good camp food, too."

"Yes. And I owe him a pair of leather gloves. Let me put these near the back of the spring, where Relic put his pack when we were up here earlier. He might be more likely to find it there."

She stood, her legs feeling the fatigue again, and

brushed herself off. Chance, ever magnanimous, gave Ash a turn at scratching her head. Hailey walked around the pool to the block of stone where the petroglyph was etched and placed the water on top. She rested her back on the rock and looked into the high cliff and the trail that had taken them to the top, searching for signs of Relic. She waited a few more minutes then walked back to Ash and Chance.

They had a lot to tell Deputy Dawson. And she had a hell of a story to write.

CHAPTER 60

She fed Chance a can of stew, slightly heated, and ate a bologna sandwich, the only food in her little apartment. She'd not had time to stock the place. With something in her stomach, she stripped and stood under a hot shower for fifteen minutes, watching the red dirt and sweat sluice from her skin, flowing down the drain in silted rivulets. She washed her hair three separate times and scrubbed until the rinse water was clear, then let the water massage her neck and back, warming her to the core.

She dried her hair with a towel and found clean clothes, the feel of them stiff and a little weird.

She looked at Chance, who sat by the only window in the small efficiency.

"Your turn," she said, returning to the tub and filling it with warm water. She coaxed her into the bathroom with a piece of bread and lifted her into the bath. Chance seemed to understand what was going on and enjoyed the scrub-down, leaning into Hailey as she rubbed soapy water against her skin. When she was done, Hailey pulled the plug and rinsed the dog with a glass of water. Chance leapt from the tub and Hailey covered her face as the dog shook herself nearly dry.

"Wish I could do that." She patted Chance between the ears.

She had a meeting with Ash and her editor, Martineau, at the newspaper office at three o'clock. Martineau and Burke had seemed to be friends, so her news about Burke would not be well received. But it had to be told. She glanced at the clock; she was running late. She brushed through her hair – no time to dry it all the way.

Chance stayed with her on their walk to the outer door of the Red Rock Sentinel and parked herself by the front window. Hailey went inside, through the swinging door at the front counter, and to a conference room in the back. Ash was sitting across the table, arms crossed, listening to Martineau. Ash wore an olive canvas shirt and cotton shorts. The guy cleans up pretty well, she thought.

"We won't make these kinds of allegations against Burke without solid sources." Martineau pointed his finger at Ash.

"We have eyewitnesses." Ash motioned toward Hailey and himself. "That whole operation out there is crooked as hell."

Hailey sat next to Ash.

"See, that's the kind of thinking that keeps you from advancing, Ash." It was Martineau's turn to cross his arms.

"What's going on?" she asked.

"I've told him the whole thing, even some of what happened to you, but he won't run a story without more."

"More what?"

"More proof." Martineau leaned toward her, his cheeks florid. "And you, dear, are out of control. No one authorized you to go snooping around the Broken Inn. Trespass! Breaking and entering! Insubordination! Your job was to interview Burke and get back here, simple and easy. You've got a whole stack of stories sitting on your desk, unwritten…"

"The story about Broken Inn will be done by tomorrow."

Martineau shook his head. "Not good enough. You're not objective anymore. You've let yourself become part of the story itself. In fact, I want your desk emptied by the end of the day."

"I'm fired?" Her eyes grew round.

They sat in silence for a moment, watching each other.

"Am I interrupting?" Dawson's voice filled the room like a gust of air.

Martineau sat back in his chair.

Hailey tried to process the fact that she'd been fired from her first real job. It was worse than that, too; her position was financed by the university externship program, so the college would know, her professors, her classmates, everyone. And she'd been fired from a position mostly free of charge to the paper. How much worse could that look on a resumé?

Dawson sat at the end of the table. "I need to get a full report from you folks," he nodded at Hailey and Ash, "down at the station."

"I've just been fired," she glared at Martineau, "so I've got plenty of time for a very full and complete report."

"You fired her?" Dawson straightened his spine, surprise in his eyes.

"That's none of your business, deputy," Martineau fired back.

"Well, maybe it isn't and maybe it is…" Dawson leaned away from the table. "You see," he turned to Hailey and Ash, "it seems that your editor, here, is the owner of the Broken Inn and the canyon south of there, Demon's Roost."

"What?" Ash's mouth dropped open.

"And, it seems, he has leased it to some supposed hotel company with ties to organized crime out of southern California."

Hailey inhaled quickly.

"So, he has an interest in the success of whatever the hell they are doing out there because, it turns out, the lease gives him one percent of the revenue."

"You don't know that…" Martineau challenged.

"The FBI has suddenly become very helpful here. And they've had an undercover operation on this for months."

They all stared at the editor.

Martineau's cheeks turned a deep shade of purple.

"So," Dawson turned toward Hailey, "if he's firing you to cover up his own role in all of this, that could be a criminal act." Dawson placed his hands on his belt, a subtle reminder of his authority.

"Holy crap." Hailey stared at Martineau, who kept his lips clamped shut.

"Mrs. Sauts will be really, really interested in this," Ash nodded, glancing between Dawson and Martineau.

"Who's Mrs. Sauts?" Hailey asked.

"The owner of the Red Rock Sentinel."

CHAPTER 61

Chance met them outside the storefront, spun two quick turns, and followed them to the sheriff's office. Hailey and Ash gave a full account of events to Deputy Dawson, who seemed especially curious about the man who'd helped Hailey out of Bitterbrush Canyon, the man he'd asked about when she first met with the deputy. She said he'd called himself "Ralph" or "Relish" or such, refused to talk to her other than through simple instructions, and mumbled incoherently most of the time.

"Black hair? Ponytail?" Dawson asked.

"Well, yes," she admitted, quickly wishing she hadn't.

"Been looking for that character for a while, now."

"Oh. The bigfoot you've been searching for?"

"You remembered." He scratched his chin. "I don't know if that's who it is or not…"

She shrugged and explained that after the man

helped her up the cliff, he was on his way, away from the old inn. Dawson asked, but she said they didn't know who had caused the chaos of the fire and the crashing water tower. She didn't think Dawson was completely convinced, but eventually he let it go, focusing on more critical events. When she asked about the FBI investigation, and Martineau's lease of the inn, Dawson was much more evasive than he'd been in the editor's office, neither confirming nor denying any of it. They shared a smile at that point, a tacit agreement that he would not press farther on the subject of Relic and she'd not press farther about an on-going federal investigation. She agreed to write up a narrative in the next day or so and bring it to him. When they were finally done, she and Ash left the room where they'd been interviewed and walked to the City Park, just a few yards away.

They found a bench under a boxelder tree, and Chance inserted herself between them, allowing each an equal opportunity to pay her some attention.

"Eddie Martineau owns the Broken Inn." Ash shook his head. "I'd have never guessed…"

"In a deal with organized crime." Hailey rubbed Chance's ears.

"Some of those guys don't give you much of a choice. I mean, if they wanted to use Demon's Roost,

Martineau could hardly refuse."

"Maybe. But then he promoted Broken Inn like crazy, the whole new tourism project, like his wallet depended on it." She looked at Ash.

"Yeah. He could have gone to the feds instead and helped them with their investigation. But he didn't."

"Judging from the reaction we got from the deputy," she pointed behind her, "Martineau knew exactly who he was getting into bed with."

They watched Chance eyeing the coffee shop across the street, the sweet smell of cinnamon rolls drifting toward them.

"I'm glad I don't work for him anymore," she said.

"Mrs. Sauts is not going to be happy about this." Ash raised a finger in the air. "She's likely to can Martineau. In a flash."

"Wow. Well, I won't be the only one without a job."

"Maybe. Maybe not." A nascent grin formed on his lips.

"What?"

"Last year, when Martineau was out sick for a few weeks, Mrs. Sauts made me associate editor."

"Really?"

"I never liked working for him, so when he came back, I renegotiated my deal. I wanted to be a whitewater rafting guide, so I did that and became a contract photographer in between trips and off-season. That way, Martineau couldn't lord over me as much. I could tell him when I was and wasn't available and I worked independently. No time clocks or schedules. I just sent him a little bill every month for my work."

"You were associate editor?"

"Don't look so surprised. I have my BA in journalism."

"So…"

"Yeah, my point is, I may be associate editor again, for a few weeks anyway. In which case, we're going to need a seasoned reporter right away, and I know a good one." He nodded at her.

"I don't know about that…"

"It may be temporary, but…"

"I'd take it."

"If we can't get your article published in the paper, we'll use the blog."

"*Our* article," she corrected.

"Either way, we'll get it out there."

"Making injustice visible," she said to herself.

Chance laid her head on Hailey's lap and stared up at her, the whites of her eyes like crescent moons.

"Hey, would you show me how to go rock climbing sometime?"

"Of course." He smiled.

"And I'm looking forward to that Mexican dinner you promised." She cleared her throat. "But first, we have a couple other things to take care of."

CHAPTER 62

Hailey, Ash, and Chance had stocked up at Addison's IGA. Dog food was first on the list. She'd found a pair of work gloves to replace the one of Relic's that she'd lost on the cliffs. They'd loaded their cart with three different flavors of beef jerky, a loaf of French bread, two squeeze bottles of strawberry jam, fruit cocktail snacks, a fifth of blended Kentucky bourbon, and a jumbo bag of peanut M&Ms. They stuffed it all into a new nylon daypack.

Hardly enough to thank the wandering recluse, but a start.

Ash took them all to the Broken Inn, driving his pickup close to Sakwa Spring. They parked and went to a spot overlooking the project. The ruined water tower and its supporting struts were still smeared out below the bulldozer, pine blocks and pixie sticks tangled under a collapsed wall like a cyclone had hit it. The earth mover remained on its side, mortally wounded and half-covered in dirt by men who'd doused the smoldering water pump that had burned in the dozer's bucket. Yellow police tape circled the whole mess, an attempt to keep the curious at bay, and it made the scene oddly tidy, as if the disaster was an organized part of the project, planned from the beginning.

An eerie silence swept in with the breeze, a quiet so radically different from just a couple of days ago it seemed as if they'd time-travelled to a distant future.

"I'm going to put this next to the petroglyph, on the far side of the spring," Hailey lifted the pack. "Give me a minute?"

"Sure. Good idea," Ash agreed.

She carried it to the place she'd left the bottles of water two days ago. They were gone, so she assumed that Relic had found and taken them.

"Good," she said to herself. "I hope you find this, too." She placed the pack where the bottles had been and looked up the narrow trail, up along the rim, checking to see if Relic was in view.

He may be watching, she thought, but staying out of sight. Or maybe he was long gone, traversing the plateau or exploring the cliffs in some distant canyon. She sat on the ground and examined the little spring, the sheen of the water, its cattails straighter and stronger than they'd been the last time she was there.

She thought about something Relic had said: that a long life may or may not be good enough, but a good life was always long enough. Mom had lived a good life, a life that really was long enough. And what about herself? She'd been living a good life, too, these last few days, as hard and scary and relentless as they had been. A better life than she'd lived in quite a while.

Her mother would want her memory to be natural, not obsessive, to bring a smile, not a tear. Well, the tear will come with the smile for a long time, she thought, but something about this country helps – its stark reality, its off-planet cliffs and spires, rock formations that defy logic, contradictions of color. Every bend in the trail offers whole new perspectives, swells and canyons and bluffs, the bones of the earth laid bare. Maybe that was part of its magic – the upending of one's perspective.

And right here was Relic's little spring, she thought, patting the rock beneath her. An oasis. Home to cattails and lizards, frogs and falcons, water snakes and coyotes. And moonshining hermits.

She imagined the heartbeat of the earth, thumping every twenty-six seconds.

A loneliness in her had eased. She knew now that

she would stay in this rugged country, her and her new pals. And whatever the old guard did at the town newspaper, she and Ash would move forward with their own style of investigative reporting. Channeling her anger. Her mother would be proud.

She realized that Relic had been doing the same sort of thing; he'd been protecting Sakwa Spring all along, channeling his anger at the stupidity of those who were destroying it. In his own way, he was helping the oasis to heal, doing something just and fair, doing it actively and purposefully. That was what she would be doing too, from now on, in her mother's memory but for herself, too. Refocused. Guiding her own thoughts, her own life.

"What you think, you become. What you feel, you attract. What you imagine, you create," she whispered.

She glanced one last time at the distant ridge and saw a flash of light, so quick she had to assure herself she'd seen it, but she knew it was Relic, caveman of the canyons, watching out for the living beings in these special places.

She knew just how to write the story.

AUTHOR'S NOTE AND ACKNOWLEDGEMENTS

Thank you for reading *Broken Inn* – I really hope you enjoyed it! As an author, I depend heavily on book reviews and referrals. So, if you think others might enjoy the novel, too, please leave a quick review on Amazon and any other internet site you use for selecting books to read. *The moment it takes to leave a quick book rating makes a lasting difference for the author!*

It is true that the earth is pulsating every 26 seconds, though not all seismologists agree why. Personally, I like Relic's explanation best.

Hailey wonders why, at one point, so many place names in the western backcountry include references to purgatory. "Hell Roaring Canyon" is an actual canyon along the Green River, named by John Wesley Powell. "Devil's Tail" (*Diamonds of Devil's Tail*) and "Demon's Roost" (*Broken Inn*) are fictional places that reflect the character of the very real gorges, cliffs, and rock formations throughout Canyonlands National Park.

I eagerly acknowledge my parents, family, colleagues, and many accomplices. Though way too many to recognize all of them, the names of a few have been used in the story – place names, business names, or such

— as a quick "shout out" to those fine people, who deserve a lot more.

Thanks to all who understand their kinship with the planet and those who work in the service of their ideals.

Thanks also to all my family and friends who have shared canoes and rafts with me over the decades: Gina, Sarah, Adam, Sarajean, Nate, Doug, Dave, Ron, Jeff, Bridger, and many others. The rivers of this nation deserve and depend on our respect and preservation. Their waters are sacred.

As always, I thank Jim Dempsey, at Novel Gazing, for his careful attention to detail and insightful suggestions. Thanks to Nate Granzow of Venator Media Solutions for excellent comments on the first few chapters. And special thanks to Sarah Reilley for her edits throughout. Thanks also to Dad and Gina for their solid editing suggestions and to Gina for letting me disappear for hours and days at a time while working on this effort. And I thank Nate again for the incredible map art at the front of the book.

Thanks to Daniel Thiede for the fabulous cover art and text layout!

And, finally, I thank the many people who have inspired the characters in this work.

The roar of whitewater drowned out all other sounds of life, even Ethan's own breathing. He watched with a sense of awe as Anya powered her boat to the left, deftly guiding it as she watched the rapids on their right.

Ethan followed her move, paddling to line up with the left shore, then rowing toward it.

In mere moments, a huge rock appeared on their right, the river bellowing over it like a jet engine. Water reared high above the rock, spraying whitecaps into the air, plunging into a crater of water below, swirling and rising and collapsing on itself as it went. He could feel the waves rocking his raft even several yards away. As quickly as the sound had engulfed him, it started to fade.

"Ethan!" Anya yelled across, her voice a mere reminder among the sound of throbbing rapids to look up, pay attention.

He saw her rowing toward the right shore. Quickly, he spun the raft so his back was to the same shore and began to row.

The current was much faster here than in the stretch of flat water he'd gotten used to. He could hear and sense the rapids directly in front of him. He dipped the oars and pulled mightily with mediocre results. He forced himself to row faster and harder, desperate to avoid the coming whitewater.

The sound of the first rapid he'd passed was nothing compared to the vibration and roar of the waves ahead. All he could do was keep rowing, putting his legs into it, straining his back against the oars.

Without warning, the front of his raft dipped sideways into a trough, nearly tossing him out of the boat. His upriver oar swung through thin air, angled out of the water. He leveled out for a moment, bracing himself, then the raft buckled inward as it crashed into a wave ten feet above his head. His fingers slipped from the oars and found brief purchase on the center frame. The river pounded him like a waterfall and he lost all sense of direction as the raft spun high on the cresting water, spray blasting his skin like shotgun pellets.

The raft slid sideways across the downriver slope of the high wave. He was weightless for a moment as it fell toward another trough and then, at the bottom, the raft buckled again, tossing him clear of the boat like a piece of cork.

He had time for only half a breath before the cold water sucked him under, spinning him down through the roiling currents. He struggled for a second, flailing his arms and legs, then stopped. As water pressure began to hurt his ears, he knew he was too deep to swim up, that he'd use his air too quickly if he tried to fight the current. Let the life jacket do its job, he thought, if it can. He forced himself to relax, to conserve his energy, to let the river take him where it would. To do that, he had to surrender - fully, unconditionally – to the power of the water, the flow of rain, snowmelt, and desert springs all merged into one gargantuan muscle of river tearing through bedrock itself, carving grand canyons out of solid stone. What could anyone do against that?

His arms and legs tingled painfully then went numb - from the cold or lack of oxygen he could not tell. His mind flashed to Relic's water bottle. Water, the one thing he could not live without in this harsh and beautiful desert; the one thing that would now kill him. He would never take water for granted again.

Though his eyes were closed, stars and spears of light flashed across them. He spun more slowly than before but disorientation had seized control. Was he right side up? Rising? Sinking?

His chest burned like molten magma, cooking and crackling, dying for a simple gasp of air to release the flame. His muscles moved involuntarily to expel his breath but he forced them back. He knew he had to breathe, and soon, even if it meant sucking his lungs full of water, but he rallied back against the thought, squeezing it out, willing himself to never breathe again. When his throat convulsed, the world became a void.

The tent became a dome of light, then began to smolder and burst into flame near the back, near the kitchen stove.

"Hey, we just cleaned the grill back there," Relic said, making Wyatt laugh.

The fire spread slowly, casting a halo of light across the camp. Security guards hollered, workers yelled their curses and questions, and everyone rushed to see what the commotion was all about.

"Is she really crazy enough to do that?" Wyatt asked.

"Yep," Relic nodded.

"Well, shee-it," Wyatt did his best imitation of Faye.

Relic smiled. "Don't let her hear you or she'll knock your block off."

"No doubt."

"Would you see what you can do to slow down that backhoe up ahead of us and anything else with a lock and key? Then work your way north, swing back toward the staircase and we can meet up there."

Wyatt nodded.

"Keep a close look out. They'll be searching as soon as the mess [kitchen tent] is under control."

"What's your next move?" Wyatt asked.

Relic jerked his thumb toward the portable toilets. "Really?" Wyatt said.

Relic turned and faded into the dark. Wyatt heard footfalls, someone moving quickly toward him. After a moment, he recognized her shape bobbing along. She tossed something and he heard it clacking into the bed of a pickup. She nearly ran into him.

"Hey." He put his hands out toward her.

"Hey," she said, slowing, but only a bit. "Here." She tossed a stick of dynamite to him, the fuse sparkling lit.

"Shit!"

"Throw it!" she shouted as she ran past. "Now!"

Wyatt stared at the tube in his hand. The fuse sputtered and spat and shortened with every second, time compressed with the tightness of his breath, the glowing fuse moving forward immutably until something like a spinning clutch popped in his chest and muscle movement became possible again. He reached his arm back and threw it as far and as fast as he could, then he spun and ran to the side of another truck and turned back to look.

The pickup Faye had tossed something into rose into the air with a smack that washed away all other sound, then fell back to the ground with a nasty twist as pieces of sheet metal dropped from the sky.

"Holy…"

Wyatt's stick of dynamite exploded somewhere beyond another truck, lighting something on fire, sending a second sonic boom through his skull, making him jump in his tracks. He stared at the blaze as it settled into a steady burn and looked the direction Faye had run.

A third, fourth, and fifth explosion erupted in quick succession in the row of portable toilets and Wyatt knew it was Relic's work. Where was Relic's peaceful resistance now? Lord, he hoped no one was in those toilets. Then, he thought, what a mess of shit, and he giggled and smacked his hands together.

Oh, my god, was it possible to have so much fun? He never expected stopping Lord Winnieship from stealing this canyon to feel so damn good.

He stared at the fire he'd started and tried to think. He wanted to follow Faye but there was no telling what other mayhem she had in mind, and he did not want to walk into an exploding outhouse. He tried to regulate his breathing, with only a little luck. He circled away from the path Faye had taken, giving her a wide berth, moving to the outer edge of the parked vehicles.

Wyatt turned and trotted toward a lone backhoe, maybe sixty yards away. Though the electric lights of the compound were out, the kitchen and dining room blaze cast a sallow glow on the tops of the other tents and equipment. The upper arm of the yellow backhoe was lit like a candle.

His shins scraped across brittle sage and he slowed to a walk. He'd lost his own toothpicks, so that trick [of jamming the locks] would not work with the heavy equipment. After Faye's dynamite, toothpicks seemed pretty pathetic anyway. Maybe there was a set of keys kept in the ignition that he could toss away. Or maybe he could flatten its tires or pull wires from under the dash to disable the beast. He turned to watch the bobbing of flashlights all around the burning mess tent a quarter of a mile away. The voices of men rose and fell in a rhythm that was almost musical, like an offbeat composition.

He stopped at the base of the backhoe and stared up at the top, where the boom and dipper attached. He circled the machine to the open cabin and peered inside.

"Stop and turn around." The voice was deep and familiar.

Wyatt turned and raised his hands. Even in the semi-dark, Lynch's muscled bulk identified him immediately. He held a pistol aimed at Wyatt's chest.

"You!" Lynch said. "You sonofabitch."

Wyatt saw the left hook a milli-second before it struck his jaw, wrenching his head away and toward the ground. He stumbled to the side. A blow to his stomach struck like a rocket and his chest ached, all the veins in his body shut down by a sonic boom. Slivers of light flashed through his eyes, closed tight against the assault. He sensed himself floating to the earth, his muscles turned to liquid. He was out before he hit the dirt.

Owen thought his heart had completely halted, and it had, for just a second, and then it began a pounding, deep and strained, pumping blood through his temple in spurts then galloping quickly, flushing his cheeks.

Holy flying eff.

He sucked a shallow breath of air, pulled his gaze from the dead arm, and looked back the way he'd come. From this perspective, the arm was well-hidden on the backside of the long pile of dirt, tucked close to the low rock face and well out of view from the hangar and the tents beyond. Last night's heavy storm had flushed loose soil from the canyon slopes and probably from the body, too. He tried not to look back at the fragile hand, but he couldn't help himself. Skin shriveled against the tiny bones, stiff leather holding the assembly of joints together, keeping the fingers pointed in confusing, haphazard directions, their owner not sure which way to go. Red nail polish added a cheap party flare, a celebration completely out of place.

Holy eff. Hold it together, he told himself, get back to camp and pretend he'd never seen it. Tell Thomas. No one else. Someone here could have killed this girl, must have killed her. Why? What had happened here?

He turned his eyes to his feet and shuffled across the ground, moving to the edge of the pile of dirt. He peered around the mound and saw the edge of the hangar and the back of the tents. No one seemed to be around, so he hustled away from the dirt, across the hard-packed surface, and into the hangar. He went to the yellow plane again and leaned on the right strut, his breath still shallow and labored.

Owen looked beyond the hangar to the field outside and the Cessna waiting for them. Where was Thomas?

"Did you get that cold drink?"

Panic charged through his brain, a devil's hot wire crackling from one ear to the other. His head jerked toward the front of the plane and he clamped his hands tightly on the strut. Everett's question was smooth but – was there an undertone in his voice?

Owen managed to force a breath.

"No…" he patted the wing support, glanced at Everett, then spoke to the plane itself, too nervous to look at the man again. Squeezing the strut helped him to focus. "I got sidetracked by this old Aeronca. What year is it, do you know?"

"1946, I'm told."

"Oh."

"Are you a pilot?" Everett moved out of the sunlight and into the shade of the hangar. Owen knew the man could see him better now.

"No, no, I'm not. Tried to take some lessons, but…" He struggled to keep his thoughts on the aircraft, away from what he'd discovered. "Just look at this panel, the instrument panel," he pointed. "Not hardly any instruments here, though. It's all metal, too, like the dashboards on old cars." He kept his eyes on the cockpit, still reluctant to look directly at Everett.

"Yeah, I've looked it over myself." Everett's voice seemed more normal now, more conversational. "The owner has a friend who came out here a couple of days ago. He's restoring the old bird, but I don't know how far he's gotten. The fabric looks like a stiff breeze would pull it off." He ran his hand across the edge of the wing opposite Owen. "You wouldn't catch me flying in this death trap." Everett wandered away from the plane, plucked a long blade of grass from the ground and began to twist it absentmindedly.

"Yeah, the cloth on this one needs completely replaced." Owen tried to sound like an authority on the subject and felt his nerves calm a little as he spoke. He ducked under the wing and walked into the sunlight.

"Seen my boss?"

"I think he's about done," Everett pointed toward the tents along Ghost Creek. Thomas and Angela were walking slowly back toward the Cessna. Angela was explaining something, Thomas nodding.

"Well, it was nice meeting you." Everett moved quickly toward Owen and offered his hand, his smile show-room friendly, his shake cold and curt.

"Yes. Nice meeting you, too." Owen made eye contact briefly and turned back toward the Cessna. "Better get going."

He strode toward the rented Park Service plane, muscle memory moving his legs, thoughts flowing back to that tortured hand, its ragged movement in the breeze. He tried to be nonchalant about getting the hell out of there. Angela and Thomas came closer to the Cessna.

"Got what we need?" Owen asked Thomas.

Thomas looked up. "Yep. Thanks for the tour and good luck to you," he said to Angela. He shook hands with her and Everett and turned back to the plane.

Owen did not wait to be told to climb in. He adjusted his seatbelt, put the headset on, and waited. Thomas did the same.

How was he going to tell Thomas about the dead girl's arm? When should he tell him? Angela and Everett positioned themselves to one side and in front of the Cessna. They could see any conversation between him and Thomas, so he stayed quiet.

Thomas spent a moment examining the air map and checking the instruments. Out of the corner of his eye, Owen saw the man with the red hat, Luke, run up to Everett and whisper urgently in his ear. Everett glared at the plane, then gave some sort of order to Luke, who ran out of view. Did they know he'd found the girl's body?

"Clear prop!" Thomas pumped the throttle and turned the key, the engine spitting to life. Owen sat back in his seat, eyes straight ahead, and listened to the engine as Thomas adjusted the fuel mixture and checked the magnetos, turning first one off, then the other, then both back on for flight, Owen wishing he would hurry the hell up. Thomas finally pushed the throttle forward and the engine roared, the Cessna shuddered, and they began to roll down the dirt strip, vibrating, bouncing, jarring over small ruts until suddenly, liftoff, and the ride became smooth and even, the engine solid and throaty, clear air ahead of them, and Owen finally took a deep breath.

Thomas made a gentle turn to their left, flying back toward the creek, the dig site, and the old hangar, circling to gain altitude needed to fly over the plateau above the camp. They rose steadily as they went, Owen thinking how to explain what he'd found, hoping he'd done the right thing by waiting until they were in the air, bound for home base.

They leveled out about two miles past the Quonset hut, aiming for the broad Colorado River as they continued to climb beyond the canyon. A ribbon of dust rose to their right, a truck in motion along the road, soon to be well behind them. Ghost Creek faded from view as they neared the level of the plateau. They could see the bronze river beyond as it wound its way southward, on toward the Grand Canyon, on to the Gulf of California. Owen rubbed his hands on his pants and readied himself.

"Thomas," he spoke into the microphone on his headset.

"Yes?"

"I've got something to tell you, something I discovered down there while you were with the archeologist..."

"Yes?" Thomas checked his GPS and adjusted his heading.

Just then, a hollow thump jarred Thomas forward and he pushed the yoke in, then tugged and released it as he slumped back in his seat. Owen grabbed the yoke and his eyes swelled wide and he stared at Thomas' slackened face and began to scream his name, bobbing the plane's nose up, down, up, when another hollow thump jarred them and oil sprayed into the air and onto the right side of the windshield and he heard the motor cough, and cough again, and felt the Cessna lose its power, dropping in the air, descending toward the ground and he screamed again.

"Wicked chickens lay deviled eggs, but this one's rotten, too." Relic took the binoculars from his eyes and stroked his buffalo-beard goatee. Something about the man on the trail below made his skin tingle.

He slid away from the edge, out of the man's line of sight, and looked about. An unlikely descendant from clans of the Hopi and Scottish, Relic wandered the remote reaches of the Green and Colorado Rivers and the high plateaus between them, a weathered hermit at home in the desert outback, roaming ancient trails, brewing his homemade gin at a couple of narrow, spring-fed crags tucked above the floodplains. He tightened his ponytail, errant strands of white flashing through his coal-black hair.

A dried-out branch of cottonwood leaned against the nearest in a row of six Pueblo houses nestled tightly between the floor and ceiling of the cliff, a string of separate rooms, their stone blocks still mortared together in the corners. Inside were mano stones, held in the hand for grinding corn, and metate, wide-bottom slabs used for the same purpose. A child's bow and arrow, chert for making knives and arrowheads, and bowls of corn, squash, and other seeds were set neatly on indoor ledges under a layer of dust; their owners, it seemed, only away for the winter. In the farthest room were a row of large pots painted with white and black bolts of lightning, edges curved and sharp, with handles on their sides, tops still sealed tight, their contents a thousand year-old mystery. Relic meant to keep it that way.

He leaned forward again. The man strode purposefully toward the high cliff with something long, something strangely out of place, glinting in the desert sun. He put the binoculars back to his eyes.

Of all the things to be lugging in this remote country, to be balancing on bony shoulders in the noonday heat, that angular, outrageous shape was an aluminum ladder, designed for the suburban handyman.

"Well, shit on a shingle." Relic tucked the binoculars away, lay flat near the ruins, and waited.

The man struggled awkwardly up the trail, finally dragging the extension ladder to a stop at the base of the sandstone cliff. He wiped the sweat from his forehead and gazed upward at the solid, sloping rock and the extreme measures the Pueblo people had taken to keep their houses and granaries hidden and safe, high in the cliffs and crags, deep in the desert outback. Centuries ago, they carried masonry, mortar, and jars of water up rickety, wooden ladders to build these solid structures; hard, hot work with just one purpose – protection against interlopers. Now the man below had a ladder of his own, and he rested it against the stone and tugged on the rope that extended it upward, the arms squealing in their tracks, each rung clunking into place as it went.

The man shifted an empty duffle bag across his shoulders and began climbing carefully, one step at a time.

The twenty-eight foot ladder shifted suddenly an inch to the side, but it seemed to find a new, more solid base. The man flexed his knees, testing to make sure the aluminum would not slide any farther, and glanced up. The top of the ladder reached just above the lip of the sandstone ledge.

That man must think he'll find a load of artifacts up here, Relic thought, maybe even lower them to the ground by rope from the ruins, then step back down the ladder unencumbered. But the ancient Pueblo had one last line of defense.

Relic rolled away from the ruins and shifted along the ledge until he was directly in front of the top rung of the ladder, waiting. He listened as the man placed one hand on the step above him, then the next, one at a time, rising cautiously higher.

The man reached the cap of the ledge, but when he looked across the level shelf, where the stone walls rested, there, alone in the red dust, sat Relic looking, he knew, like a weathered Pueblo man, a ghost of the ruins, with a black goatee and a pony tail, holding a three foot cottonwood branch as thick as his arm.

"Shit!" the man's foot slid off one rung and down to the next. "Holy mother…who the hell are you?"

Relic's dark eyes squinted, his lips rose at the corners, and he slid the branch toward the man's ladder.

"What the hell?" the man tightened his grip.

Relic placed the branch on the top rung and began to push.

"No! Shit, no!" He raised his hand for a flash then returned it to the ladder. "You'll kill me!"

Relic slowly pushed the ladder away from the ledge, forcing it to twist outward on one end, then the other, as it lifted from the face of the cliff.

The man dropped both feet to the lower rung and slid his hands quickly down the aluminum sides, dropping his feet, holding for a moment, dropping, holding, dropping as the ladder leaned farther and farther away from the cliff, more and more upright above, ready to catapult him into a pile of rocks, and just as his feet hit the dirt the ladder tipped past its balance, dipped overhead and spun out of his hands and onto the rocky ground with a *clang*, a bounce, and another *clang!*

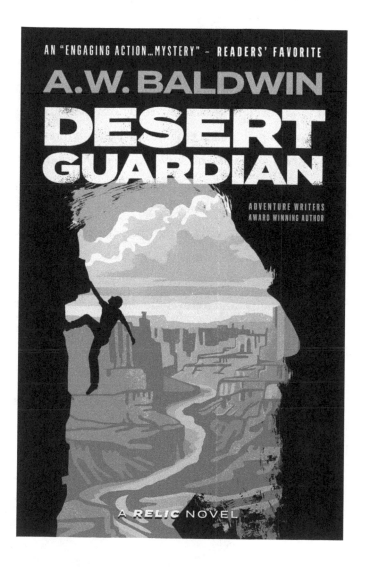

A moonshining hermit.
A campus bookworm.
A midnight murder.

Ethan's world turns upside-down when he slips off the edge of red-rock cliffs into a world of twisting ravines and coveted artifacts. Saved by a mysterious desert recluse named Relic, Ethan must join a whitewater rafting group and make his way back to civilization. But someone in the gorge is killing to protect their illegal dig for ancient treasures... When Anya, the lead whitewater guide, is attacked, he must divert the killer into the dark canyon night, but his most deadly pursuer is not who he thinks... Ethan struggles to save his new friends, face his own mortality, and unravel the chilling murders. But when they flee the secluded canyon, a lethal hunter is hot on their trail…

Can an unlikely duo and a whitewater crew save themselves and an ancient Aztec battlefield from deadly looters?

Readers' Favorite says:

Desert Guardian is an "engaging action... mystery"

The novel features "tough, credible characters"

Readers' Favorite Five Star Review

Buy now from a bookstore near you or ***amazon.com***

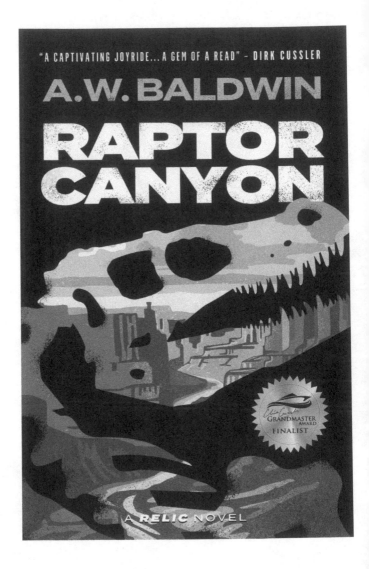

"A CAPTIVATING JOYRIDE... A GEM OF A READ" – DIRK CUSSLER

A.W. BALDWIN

RAPTOR CANYON

GRANDMASTER AWARD FINALIST

A *RELIC* NOVEL

A moonshining hermit.
A big-city lawyer.
A $35million con job.

An impromptu murder leads a hermit named Relic to an unlikely set of dinosaur petroglyphs and to swindlers using the unique rock art to turn the canyon into a high-end tourist trap. Attorney Wyatt and his boss travel to the site to approve the next phase of financing, but his boss is not what he seems... When a treacherous security chief tries to kill Relic, Wyatt is caught in the deadly chase. The mismatched pair must tolerate each other while fleeing through white-water rapids, remote gorges, and hidden caverns. Relic devises a plan to save the treasured canyon, but Wyatt must come to terms with the cost to his career if he fights his powerful boss... A college student with secret ties to the site, Faye joins the kitchen crew so she can spy on the enigmatic project. When she hears Relic's desperate plan, she has a decision to make...

Armed with a full box of toothpicks (and a little dynamite), can the unlikely trio monkey-wrench the corrupt land deal and recast the fate of Raptor Canyon?

"A RETURN OF THE MYSTERIOUS HERMIT RELIC... A PAGE-TURNING THRILLER" - DIRK CUSSLER

A.W. BALDWIN

WINGS OVER GHOST CREEK

ADVENTURE WRITERS AWARD WINNING AUTHOR

ADVENTURE WRITERS COMPETITION FINALIST 2020

A *RELIC* NOVEL

A moonshining hermit.
A reluctant pilot.
A $5million plunder.

Owen discovers a murdered corpse at a college-run archeological dig in the Utah outback but when he and a park service pilot try to reach the sheriff for help, their plane is shot from the sky. Owen must ditch the aircraft in the Colorado River, where he is saved by a gin-brewing recluse named Relic. The offbeat pair flee from the sniper and circle back to warn the students but not everyone there is who they seem... The two must trek through rugged canyon country, unravel a baffling mystery, and foil a remarkable form of thievery. Suzy, a student at the dig, helps spearhead their escape but the unique team of crooks has a surprise for them...

Can they uncover the truth and escape an archeology field class that hides assassins and dealers in black-market treasure?

"A beautifully written thriller."
   – Readers' Favorite Five Star Review

"[A] humorous, fun, and well-plotted adventure. Baldwin is a master storyteller…"

— ***Landon Beach***, Bestselling Author of *The Sail*

"Baldwin delivers another gripping Relic tale with trademark wit and deft expression. This is adventure with philosophy that keeps you nodding your head long after you've put the book down."

— ***Jacob P. Avila***, *Cave Diver*, Grand Master Adventure Writers Award Winner

Wings offers "…action-packed adventure and nerve-racking suspense, with a touch of romance and humor mixed in." Baldwin has a "gift for capturing the reader's attention at the beginning and keeping them spellbound"

— ***Onlinebookclub.org review***

Grand Master Adventure Writers' Finalist Award

BUY NOW

FROM A BOOKSTORE NEAR YOU OR AMAZON.COM

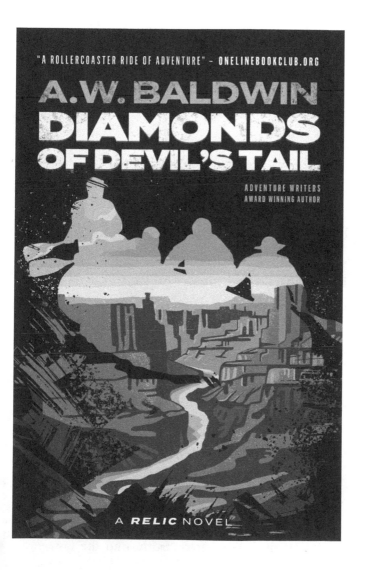

A moonshining hermit.
An English major.
A $4 million jewel heist.

When diamonds appear in a remote canyon stream, whitewater rafters and artifact thieves set off in a deadly race to the source.

Brayden, an aspiring writer, works in a Chicago insurance firm with his ambitious uncle when they embark on a wilderness whitewater adventure. On a remote hike, they find their colleague, Dylan, dead in the sand, a handful of gems in his fist. When thieves charge in, Brayden flees deeper into the canyon, where he encounters a gin-brewing recluse named Relic. Brayden's uncle is cornered and cuts a deal with the thieves, but they each have a surprise for the other... and the rafters have ideas of their own about getting rich quick... Brayden and Relic must become allies, traverse the harsh desert, and beat the thieves to the hidden gems. Brayden must confront his uncle about suspicious payments at their insurance firm and what he was really doing at the stream where Dylan was killed...

Can they discover the truth, find the lost jewels,

and protect the rafters from grenade-tossing thieves?

"…an adeptly written thriller…the excitement and tension are superb…the entire plot [is] compelling"
– *Readers' Favorite Five Star Review*

"straightforward and thrilling, with humor intermixed… Relic is a unique and intriguing character…passionately interested in preserving the ancient archeological sites and conserving the land and water…[We] enthusiastically recommend it to readers who enjoy thrillers, action-packed adventure, and crime novels."
– *Onlinebookclub.org four out of four Star Review*

"Another rollicking Relic ride from A.W. Baldwin…a bunch of double-crossing, dirt dealing, diamond thieves run into Relic's trademark wit and ingenuity. Enjoy!"
– *Jacob P. Avila*, *Cave Diver*, Grand Master Adventure Writers Award Winner

BUY NOW
FROM A BOOKSTORE NEAR YOU OR AMAZON.COM

CPSIA information can be obtained
at www.ICGtesting.com
Printed in the USA
LVHW040042190322
713544LV00001B/10